ANIMAL LIFE

ALSO BY
AUÐUR AVA ÓLAFSDÓTTIR

Butterflies in November
Hotel Silence
Miss Iceland

ANIMAL LIFE

AUÐUR AVA ÓLAFSDÓTTIR

TRANSLATED FROM THE ICELANDIC
BY BRIAN FITZGIBBON

Black Cat

New York

Animal Life was first published as *Dýralíf* by Benedikt in Iceland in 2020

First published in English by Pushkin Press in the UK in 2022

Quotation from *Waiting for Godot* by Samuel Beckett, published by
Faber and Faber Ltd.

Published simultaneously in Canada
Printed in Canada

First Grove Atlantic paperback edition: December 2022

Designed and typeset by Tetragon, London

Library of Congress Cataloging-in-Publication data is available for this title.

ISBN 978-0-8021-6016-4
eISBN 978-0-8021-6017-1

Black Cat
an imprint of Grove Atlantic
154 West 14th Street
New York, NY 10011

Distributed by Publishers Group West

groveatlantic.com

22 23 24 25 26   10 9 8 7 6 5 4 3 2 1

ANIMAL LIFE

To those who have gone before.
To those who are here now.
To those who have yet to come.

THE MOST BEAUTIFUL OF ALL WORDS

In 2013, Icelanders voted for the most beautiful word in their language. They chose a nine-lettered one, the job title of a healthcare worker, the Icelandic term for midwife: *ljósmóðir*. In its reasoning, the jury stated that the word is a composite of the two most beautiful words: *móðir* (mother) and *ljós* (light). In Icelandic midwives are also called *yfirsetukona*, *náverukona*, *jóðmóðir*, *léttakona*, *nærkona* and *ljósa*. In Danish a midwife is a *jordemor*, in Norwegian *jordmor*, Swedish *barnmorska*, Finnish *kätilö*, German *Hebamme*, Dutch *verloskundige*, Polish *położna*, French *sage-femme*, Italian *ostetrica*, Spanish *comadrona*, Portuguese *parteira*, Estonian *ämmaemand*, Latvian *vecmāte*, Lithuanian *akušerė*, Russian *акушерка*, Yiddish אַקושערקע, Irish *cnáimhseach*, Welsh *bydwraig*, Arabic قابلة, Hebrew מיילדת, Catalan *llevadora*, Hungarian *szülésznő*, Albanian *mami*, Basque *emagina*, Croatian *primalja*, Czech *porodní asistentka*, Chinese 助产士, Romanian *moașă* and Greek *μαία*. The meanings and origins of these words are not always clear, but in most cases they refer to a woman who helps another woman to deliver a baby into the world. The etymology in numerous languages indicates that it refers to an older woman who could be the child's maternal grandmother.

CONTENTS

I

Mother of Light

"I know not who put me into the world, nor what the world is,
nor what I myself am. I am in terrible ignorance of everything.
I know not what my body is, nor my senses, nor my soul,
not even that part of me which thinks what I say,
which reflects on all and on itself,
and knows itself no more than the rest."

BLAISE PASCAL

I receive the baby when it is born, raise it up
from the ground and present it to the world

In order to be able to die, a human first has to be born.

It is almost noon when the Arctic night finally begins to dissolve and the ball of fire rises over the horizon, or just about, a pink streak piercing through a slit in the curtains of the delivery room, barely wider than a pocket comb, landing on the suffering woman on the bed. She raises one arm, opens her palm and grabs the light, then lets her arm sink again. She has half a kiwi, laden with seeds, tattooed onto her taut belly, as if the fruit had been sliced in two with a sharp knife, but cracks have appeared in the ink and the inscription under the image has also started to stretch: Y o u r s   e t e r n a l l y . When the baby is born, the hairy fruit will shrivel up.

I slip on a mask and put on my protective gown.

The moment has arrived.

A human's most difficult experience.

To be born.

The crown emerges and shortly after I'm holding a small, slithery body covered in blood.

It's a boy.

He doesn't know who he is, or who delivered him into this world, or what this world is.

The father puts down his phone to cut the umbilical cord; with trembling hands he severs the thread between mother and child.

The mother turns her head to the side and watches.

Is he drawing a breath?

The baby draws a breath.

And I think: From now on he will draw a breath twenty-three thousand times a day.

I place the bundle of bawling flesh on the scales. The baby waves its arms about, there are no walls any more, no borders, nothing that delimits the world—it has become an unknown vastness, infinite space, unexplored land mass—it plummets through it in free fall, then calms down, its face is wrinkled, transfigured by anxieties.

The thermometer on the window ledge outside reads minus four degrees and the most vulnerable animal on earth lies in the balance, naked and helpless; it has no feathers or fur to cover itself, no scales, no body hair, only soft down on the crown of its head where the blue fluorescent light shines through.

The baby opens its eyes for the first time.

And sees the light.

It doesn't know it was being born.

I say, Welcome, mister.

I dry his wet head and wrap him in a towel, then I place him in the arms of his father, who wears a T-shirt inscribed *World's Best Dad*.

He's in turmoil and crying. It's done. The mother is exhausted and cries as well.

The man bends down with the newborn and places it carefully in the bed beside the woman. The baby turns its head towards the mother and looks at her, his eyes are still full of darkness from the depths of the earth.

He doesn't know yet that she is his mother.

The mother looks at the child and strokes its cheek with her finger. It opens its mouth. It doesn't know why it is here any more than anywhere else.

"He's got red hair like Mom," I hear the woman say.

It's their third son.

"They were all born in December," says the father.

I receive the baby when it is born, raise it up from the ground and present it to the world. I'm the mother of light. I'm the most beautiful word in our language—*ljósmóðir*.

Three minutes

When I've sewn two stitches I leave the parents alone with the baby for a while. If it isn't too windy to open the door at the end of the corridor, sometimes, between births, I step out onto the small balcony that overlooks the Miklubraut road.

There are nine delivery rooms on the ward and I normally deliver one baby a day, although it can sometimes be as many as three in the peak season. They are sometimes born in the cafeteria, in the waiting room, even in the elevator up to the maternity ward. I once ran out to the parking lot and delivered the child of a terrified young couple on the passenger seat of an old Volvo. When I've spent a long day handling blood and flesh, I'm grateful for the celestial vault when I step onto the balcony.

I take a deep breath and fill my lungs with cold air. "She's getting some fresh air," my colleagues tell each other.

Over the past weeks the weather has fluctuated a great deal.

At the beginning of the month, temperatures were in the double digits, nature had started to reawaken, buds were appearing in the trees. On the fourth of December, nineteen degrees were measured at the northernmost meteorological station in the country, then it rapidly cooled; the temperature dropped by twenty degrees in a single day, and it started to snow heavily. Ploughs struggled with the snowdrifts that have piled up; the sky was heavy with snow and tree branches buckled under its weight. Cars vanished under a thick coat of whiteness and one had to wade, knee-deep, through it to get to the bins. Then it started to rain, causing immense thaws. Dams of slush formed in the rivers, which changed course and gushed over roads and meadows, leaving mud and rocks in their wake. Just a few days ago, there had been a television report about twenty horses in the south that had been trapped in the floods. The accompanying footage revealed patches of farmland like islands in the middle of the water and bedraggled horses, which one farmer said he had reached across the flooded pasture by boat. It remained to be seen what would be in the water when the flooding subsided, whether more animals would be found there.

"Nothing is the way it ought to be any more," said the farmer to the reporter in the interview.

My sister, the meteorologist, says the same.

"One hopes everything will soon get back to normal again," said the farmer.

In Ljósvallagata, the drains couldn't cope with the water from the rainstorms and several storage rooms in the basement were inundated. When I examined the damage in my cellar, I found an artificial Christmas tree and a box full of decorations from my maternal grandaunt's belongings, which I carried back up to the third floor. Following the floods, there was a severe frost and treacherously slippy black ice, and this week two women gave birth, their arms in plaster casts after stumbling. The only thing that has been constant all month is the wind. And the darkness. When I go to work it's dark and when I get home from work it's dark.

When I return inside, the new father is standing by the coffee machine in the corridor. He signals that he wants to talk to me. They're both electrical engineers, this couple.

As a colleague of mine has pointed out, there is a growing tendency now for couples to be members of the same profession: two vets, two sports newscasters, two priests, two police officers, two coaches, two poets. While the engineer chooses his coffee mix, he explains that the little one was actually scheduled to be born on the twelfth of the twelfth, on his paternal grandfather's birthday, but he delayed his arrival by over a week.

He sips at the coffee and stares down at the lino, and I sense there is something weighing upon him. When he is finished with the cup he turns to the time of birth and asks exactly how it is calculated.

"It's based on when the baby comes out," I say.

"Not when the umbilical cord is cut? Or when the baby cries?"

"No," I say and think to myself not every baby cries. Or draws a breath.

"No, the thing is I was just wondering whether it would be possible to write that he was born twelve minutes after twelve on the birth certificate instead of nine minutes after twelve. It's a difference of three minutes."

I study him.

They had arrived at the maternity ward last night and he hasn't slept much.

"It would compensate for the twelfth of the twelfth," he adds, crushing the paper cup.

I give this some thought.

20

The man is suggesting the child was unborn for the first three minutes of its life.

"I would really appreciate it," he ends up saying.

"I might have looked at the clock wrong," I say.

He throws the cup into the bin and together we walk back towards the room where the mother and son are waiting.

He halts in front of the door.

"I know Gerður wanted a daughter, even though she never let on. Women want daughters." He hesitates and then says that they had read an article about how it was possible to control the sex of the child but it was too late by then.

"It went the way it went," he says, holding out his hand and thanking me for the help. "When you think about it," the statistics buff adds, "twenty million people share the same birthday as my son."

Few things under the sun can surprise a woman
with my work experience.
Except perhaps the being himself.

It is not uncommon for the profession of midwife to run in families, from woman to woman, and I myself descend from four generations of midwives. My great-grandmother was a midwife in the north of the country in the first half of the twentieth century and my maternal grandaunt worked in the maternity ward for almost half a century. Then

21

I have a maternal aunt who is a midwife in a small village in Jutland. According to sources, a forefather of ours, Gísli Raymond Guðrúnarson, also worked as a male midwife and delivered two hundred children. It is said that Gísli, known as Nonni, not only had good hands, but was also a highly skilled blacksmith and made his own forceps and various other useful tools.

My grandaunt's spirit still hovered in the air when I started working at the maternity ward sixteen years ago. The oldest midwives remembered her well, although the number of those who worked with her is dwindling. There are still stories about her, even among those who never met her. She was known for dropping various remarks such as *Any idiot can have a baby*. More as if she were talking to herself, it was said. One of her colleagues claimed she hadn't used such harsh words, quoting her instead as having said *it's not everyone who can be a parent*. Or even that she'd said *it's not everyone who has the mettle to become a parent*. Another person alleged that she'd worded it differently and said that *a difficult individual doesn't stop being a difficult individual just because they've had a baby*. Another said that she hadn't spoken about a difficult individual but a flawed one and that she regarded self-pity as the worst fault of all. I'm told she looked for signs of it in the future parents and said that *self-pity can be visible or hidden, but it's deeply rooted in a person's nature*.

It was also said that she predicted the future of relationships, sat down with half a coffee cup in the air and a sugar cube clenched between her teeth, and swirled the hand that held the cup so that ripples formed in the liquid and said:

"They'll have another child and then divorce."

Sometimes the message was more cryptic such as *It's a weird web what they call a family.* Her fellow midwives claimed that she had little faith in relationships and none at all in marriage. One of them went even further and said that she had no faith in man. "Those were her exact words," the colleague claimed, "I don't think she had much faith in man except when he was fifty centimetres long, helpless and speechless."

If a problem arose it was said that my grandaunt's refrain was:

Few things under the sun can surprise a woman with my work experience. Except perhaps the being himself.

Those were the words she used.

It was no secret that she had a hard time accepting the radical changes in the work of midwives, as she put it, when she was middle-aged and fathers started to attend the births of their children. It must be considered quite remarkable given that it seemed natural and normal to her that men had worked as midwives in the past.

Decades of work experience tell me otherwise was her way of protesting against the organizational changes in the maternity ward. One of her colleagues told me that she had said it was an extra burden to handle the men in the room. In the period in which my grandaunt worked

23

on the ward, women's partners would only be men and the men of her generation often came straight from their offices in their suits and ties, not knowing where to hang up their coats or put down their hats, instead handing them to the midwife. Others came directly from their workshops with their hands still smeared in oil. There were complaints that she left the fathers to their own devices and preferred to concentrate on the future mothers. It was also said that a certain obstetrician had been protective of her. When I asked former colleagues of hers why my grandaunt had needed protection, I got no clear answers. I later heard rumours that she'd had an affair with this same obstetrician for decades, but I've never been able to get this confirmed.

In my experience partners often find it difficult to witness the suffering of childbirth and feel useless watching.

They stroke the woman's arm and occasionally say:

"You're doing great."

The woman in labour says the same to her partner:

"You're doing great."

The partner tells me there's nothing he can do. Or he finds it so difficult not to be able to do anything. "I don't know what I can do," he says or "I can't take it any more." Or "I didn't know that she would suffer this much." Or "I didn't know that a birth could take seventy-eight hours." And he adds, "I can never be a part of her life's experience." The woman thinks "he will never be a part of my suffering.

He doesn't know what it's like to be locked in a vice with glistening forceps clamped to your spine."

Sometimes a partner will also have fits of nausea or dizzy spells.

The women then encourage them and tell them to go out and buy a sandwich. Then they pop into the staffroom to tell us the sandwich vending machine needs refilling and I answer that it's not part of our job description to refill them. Or they order pizzas and have them delivered to delivery room 23B. A number of things would surprise my grandaunt today, such as a pizza box on the bed of a woman in labour. If the labour drags on, the partner might have to collect the older siblings from one set of grandparents and take them to the other.

To shorten the time that women spend in the ward and minimize their partners' snacking and coming and going, we advise the women to come only when there are five-minute intervals between the contractions.

I think when my grandaunt spoke about there being no room for full-grown men in the delivery room, she was in fact referring to their size, as one of her female colleagues put it, that she felt that these *big full-grown men* didn't fit into this world of suffering women and whinging, suckling babies; that the issue revolved around the size difference between a full-grown man and a newborn.

Mammals always search for the teat

Despite these rumoured quirks, being assigned to a shift with my grandaunt nevertheless proved to be popular. Her colleagues remember her not least for two reasons: her handiwork and the cakes she baked and brought into work. I recognize the descriptions of multi-tier meringue tarts which she crammed with boiled pears and peaches and cream. At the bottom there was a sponge base which she drenched in sherry. After the women had given birth, she cut a generous slice for them, made some strong coffee and served it to them on a tray. The practice back then was for women to come into the ward considerably earlier or at the first sign of contractions and to stay in the hospital for a week after a normal birth. When my grandaunt started working in the maternity ward in the middle of the last century, the midwife's main task was to tend to the baby while the mother was resting. I have met many older women who speak of births as a pleasant rest from the toils of household chores and who in particular remember being served meals in bed; one of them used the word *pampered*. They got to know the women who lay with them on the ward and friendships were formed; they put curlers into each other's hair and smoked cigarettes together and left the hospital made-up and in high heels.

While the mothers were resting, my grandaunt spent a great deal of time in the nursery with the newborns. She

26

would take the babies there once the mothers had finished breastfeeding. She would lay them on her shoulder and pace the floor, shake burps out of them, stroke their backs and speak to them in hushed tones. Then she would put them down, change their nappies and pull the blankets over them. She would then pick up the next suckling and take it to its mother, after which she put it back in its cradle, picked up another and another after another, in turn. Her old colleagues concur that she spent a lot of time in the nursery and also spoke to the newborns. As one of them put it, she prepared them for life. There were various accounts of what she said. Someone heard her say *you've come to stay here for a while.* And she is said to have added *brace yourself, it's a steep climb ahead.* Another believed she had put the baby down in the cradle and said *you will be led astray many times along the way* and wondered whether she was quoting from the Bible. One of her colleagues claimed that she was quoting poets she personally knew and heard her say *we don't know much except that soon it darkens.* And also, *we don't know much except that soon it brightens.* The latter half of the sentence varied according to the time of the year in which the child was born, depending on whether the days were lengthening or shortening, whether the nights were bright or pitch black.

One thing my grandaunt's so-called *light sisters* all agreed on was that before the mother was discharged, my grandaunt would stoop over the cradle, bid farewell to the newborn and wish it sunshine, light and warmth. To be more precise she said *may you experience many dawns and many sunsets.* Those words actually formed the core of an obituary which one of her colleagues wrote about her.

Midwives of my grandaunt's generation often spent a long time at the bedside of the future mothers while waiting for a child to be born. Most of them used the time to knit or sew. I've heard women say that the clicking of the needles had a calming effect on them. It is also said that my grandaunt gave every baby she delivered a knitted garment. According to her co-workers, it was the premature babies who got her best-quality items with the most intricate patterns; she knitted with zeal, juggling several needles at once.

When she carried the smallest newborns to their mothers with her best wishes before they were dispatched into the unknown or *God and the four winds*, as she is said to have put it, they were packed in her handiwork from head to toe, leggings, socks, a sweater and a bonnet.

Breastfeeding advisor

After my grandaunt retired she continued to work at the maternity ward on various specialized tasks. Her main one was to assist women with breastfeeding advice. She would make the women comfortable, pull up a chair beside the bed and sit. There are few accounts of what happened after that, because she wanted to be left alone with the new mothers and would close the door behind her. The rumour was that she told them not to worry because *mammals always search for the teat*. I later met some older women who told me that she mainly spoke about the light. They think of her with great affection and say she said beautiful things. But also sad things. One said that she spoke about some Pascal fellow.

Even though she had stopped delivering babies, she was sometimes fetched when a birth was beginning to drag on, then she would pull out her old stethoscope, slip it on her ears, place her hands on the woman's belly and adjust her legs, and then speak in a low, barely audible, voice. She was talking to the child. Telling it it could be born.

And that is what it did.

It was born.

"It was my handwork that did it," said my grandaunt.

Like many midwives, she decided not to bring any children of her own into this world.

My colleagues know that I was christened after my grandaunt and that I live in her apartment, that she was Dómhildur the first and that I am Dómhildur the second; Fífa and Dýja.

There is a long tradition of being named after unmarried midwives in the family, but when my sister decided to baptize her daughter as Dómhildur, she specifically pointed out that she was not being named after me but our grandaunt.

When my grandaunt died, it transpired that she had bequeathed me half of her apartment on the third floor of Ljósvallagata and left the other half of her estate to the Icelandic Association for the Protection of Animals.

"It's a logical continuation," said Mom.

What she had left in her deposit account was earmarked for the recovery unit of the Children's Hospital and was to go towards the purchase of *three lamps for the treatment of jaundiced newborns and two incubators for premature babies*, as it was written in the will.

In the sideboard which the television stands on in Ljósvallagata, there are bottles of Bristol Cream sherry, which my grandaunt received from colleagues and some mothers when she retired. I'm told she had hinted that she wouldn't have minded a bottle of sherry but instead received ten. *Thank you for all the sherry tarts*, it says on a card tied around the neck of one of the bottles. I inherited nine of them.

Man grows in the dark
like a potato

When I was in secondary school I liked to study at my grandaunt's and often went to Ljósvallagata after school. I would stay over, first on weekends, then, eventually, weekdays too. During my midwifery studies I kept one foot in her place, eventually moving in with her for my last winter at college. I was supposedly keeping an eye on her after she'd once forgotten a coffee pot on a glowing hotplate

30

while she went out to the graveyard to tend to the family plot. I accompanied her to the stores and hairdresser's and shuttled her between places in a twenty-year-old light brown Lada Sport, which she owned but no longer drove herself. Sometimes I didn't come home at night and would forget to let her know. When I'd show up the next day she'd pronounce her verdict:

"Nothing will come of it."

On the other hand, she showed considerable interest in my curriculum or what she called *newfangled* theories.

"What do they mean that the partner's odour helps the woman through painful contractions?" she once asked.

This was followed by a story about how it wasn't uncommon for future fathers to turn up at the ward with the stench of alcohol on their breath. "They used aftershave to drown the whiff of the booze," she said. *Old Spice*. That reminds me that she would also talk about the scent of newborn babies, which she said was not unlike the smell of potatoes in a potato larder: a blend of soil and a slightly sweet musty smell.

I once flaunted an old textbook example where different species of fish were used as a yardstick to draw a picture of foetal growth and spoke about tiddlers, herring, then small haddock and finally cod. I can still hear my aunt's voice as she shook her head and said, "a foetus is a foetus, man is a mammal and bipedal." Her refrain was, "I'm a midwife and I know that man grows in the dark like a potato."

When I was doing my internship in the maternity ward, she wanted to know how many babies had been born on my watch, whether there had been any natural births, assisted deliveries or C-sections. I gave her a report. When I told her of the parents who'd had twins the year before and were having another set of twins that same morning, she said:

"Then there will be four babies in nappies in that household."

I also liked to get advice from her; I'd ask and she'd answer. But the answers could be ambivalent and weren't necessarily answers to what I'd asked, for instance:

"Woman is the only mammal, Dýja dear, who isn't fertile throughout her life."

I remember her once comparing a difficult birth to prolonged torture and saying that many women would give up if they could.

"Under other circumstances you'd confess to anything just to get away from it," she added.

When women are given gas they let go and sometimes talk about things, such as how many bones they've broken, a wrist, finger or two toes, and also the circumstances under which the breaking of the bones occurred. Although they don't mention the existence of God, conception can take on a supernatural dimension and has often occurred in unusual circumstances or at a time when it wasn't supposed to be possible for a child to be conceived; sperm might have survived for a whole week waiting for ovulation, while its parents were at opposite ends of the country, with one working in the north and the other studying in the south, or one at sea and the other on land.

I remember a woman who said she longed to be a mother and to make that happen, she'd had to find a man who wanted her to be the mother of his child. She pressed the mask against her face and swallowed the nitrous oxide, then lifted the mask and said in a slurring voice:

"It took longer than I expected. In the end, it was my fellow chemistry teacher who procured me the sperm. I'd discussed the problem with him and one night he came for a visit and I put on some coffee. He went to the bathroom and when he came back he handed me the semen in a cup.

"'There you go,' he said."

The women would talk and I would nod.

The gas can cause memory loss and when I discharged the woman, she asked "Did I mention Héðin?"

Do I concern myself with the conception?

The answer to that is I don't. My job starts after the fertilization has taken place.

Nevertheless, a simple calculation proves that the babies who are born in the greatest darkness are conceived in the spring equinox when the days and night are equally long and the children who are conceived at Christmas and the New Year are born when the shadows begin to lengthen at the beginning of October.

Born to...

Before I started to work at the maternity ward, whale-singing recordings were played to help women breathe through the pain and relax between contractions. At first, cassette players were used and the midwives dealt with taking the tapes out of their cases and putting them into the devices. Then CD players replaced the cassette players in the delivery rooms, and when I graduated, there was still a considerable selection of CDs with whale singing in the maternity ward. A number of these appliances are now gathering dust in the hospital's storage room. Instead, women compile their own playlists before coming to the ward and listen to the songs on their phones through headphones. Not long ago, I delivered a wonderful eight-pound baby girl to the echo of *Born to Die* with Lana Del Rey. I couldn't help noticing that Icelandic songwriters are far less preoccupied than those of many other nations, not least the Anglo-Saxons, with the idea of man being allotted a specific fate at birth, that man's birth has a purpose, that he is born to live, to escape, to love, to lose, to fight and, last but not least, to die. When I've taken three night shifts in a row, I often can't sleep on the fourth night. Sometimes I sit at my desk and turn on the computer. One night I made a list that I printed out and hung on the fridge:

Born to Die by Lana Del Rey.

Born in a Burial Gown by Cradle of Filth.

Dyin' Since the Day I Was Born by Leslie West.

A Star is Born by Jay-Z.

Born for Greatness by Papa Roach.

Born Free by Matt Monro.

Born Free by M.I.A.

Born Free by Kid Rock.

Born This Way by Lady Gaga.

Born This Way by Thousand Foot Krutch.

Who I Was Born to Be by Susan Boyle.

I Was Born to Love You by Queen.

Born to Love You by Lanco.

Born to Be Wild by Steppenwolf.

Born to Be Wild by Sean Kingston.

Battle Born by The Killers.

Born to Run by Bruce Springsteen.

Born to Live by Marianne Faithfull.

Born to be Alive by Patrick Hernandez.

Born to Lose by The Devil Wears Prada.

Born to Lose by Sleigh Bells.

Born Slippy by Underworld.

Born Slippy by Albert Hammond Jr.

Born Again by Newsboys.

Get Born Again by Alice in Chains.

With You I'm Born Again by Billy Preston.

Born Alone by Wilco.

Born to Be a Dancer by Kaiser Chiefs.

Born and Raised by John Mayer.

Born as Ghosts by Rage Against the Machine.

Born Cross-Eyed by Grateful Dead.

Born for This by Paramore.

Born in a Casket by Cannibal Corpse.

Born in a UFO by David Bowie.

Born in Chains by Leonard Cohen.

Born in Dissonance by Meshuggah.

Born in the Echoes by The Chemical Brothers.

Born of a Broken Man by Rage Against the Machine.

Born on the Bayou by Creedence Clearwater Revival.

Born Sinner by J. Cole.

Born to Be My Baby by Bon Jovi.

Born to Be Strangers by Richard Ashcroft.

Born to Be Wasted by 009 Sound System.

Born to Be Your Woman by Joey + Rory.

Born to Cry by Pulp.

Born to Quit by The Used.

Born to Sing by Van Morrison.

Born in the U.S.A. by Bruce Springsteen.

Born in East L.A. by Cheech & Chong.

Born to the Breed by Judy Collins.

Born to Try by Delta Goodrem.

Born too Late by The Poni-Tails.

Born too Slow by The Crystal Method.

Born Under a Bad Sign by Albert King.

Fez – Being Born by U2.
Just Born Bad by Rich Hillen Jr.
Natural Born Bugie by Humble Pie.
The Girl Who Was Born Without a Face by The Schoolyard Heroes.
There Is a Sucker Born Ev'ry Minute by Cast of Barnum.
We Weren't Born to Follow by Bon Jovi.

Then I suddenly think of a newspaper article I read not so long ago about a whale off the national coast, who sang on a different wavelength to other whales and became isolated as a result. The headline was *Lonely Whale*. While others in the group sang on the 12–25 hertz wavelength, he sang at 52 hertz, and the other whales therefore couldn't hear him.

Water of the world

Numerous other things associated with whales, apart from their singing, made their way into the maternity ward. Interest in the birth of whale calves, particularly dolphins in zoos, has resulted in a lot of women now wanting to give birth in water. For this purpose the ward has invested in five plastic birthing pools. Previously water births were very rare and only occurred in home births. Women procured themselves a plastic pool, inflated it on the living room floor and filled it with water. It took some time for many of the midwives, not least those of the older generation, to get used to handling women in the water and to seeing a baby's head emerge from below the surface. Labour can be protracted and not everyone agreed that the water was good for what my grandaunt called our working tools, our hands.

"We all sell our bodies, Dýja dear," she said, "some the brain, and others various other parts of the body."

We have discussed water births back and forth in the staffroom and come to the conclusion that, as one colleague pointed out, it is not unnatural for a child to move from one type of water to another, to grow and move in amniotic fluid and then be born into water of the world.

"Isn't the human body also mostly water?" one asked.

"Seventy per cent," another answered.

For some reason I feel as if I can hear my grandaunt's voice using the verb *splash*. *Yes, doesn't a man splash through life?* If she were in the room, she would also ask: "At what point, then, should the mother and child be fished out of the water?"

My interest in water birthing led me to read up on whale pregnancies and births and made me realize that whales and humans have a number of things in common. Like humans, whales are placental mammals and, like us, generally give birth to one offspring at a time, sometimes two. A whale, however, is only fertile once a year. The gestation period is ten to seventeen months and, like a human child, the calf is totally dependent on its mother for nourishment and protection in its first year. To feed the calf, the cow needs to lie on its side and spray milk into its mouth. Some of the larger species of calves drink up to two hundred and fifty litres of milk a day. I also discovered that calves are born tail first and that they need help to reach the surface to draw their first breath. Otherwise they would drown at birth. This means that another whale comes to help when a cow is giving birth. Whales use midwives just like humans. I was surprised to discover that no whale has the exact same caudal fin and that it was therefore like its fingerprint. I also hadn't exactly thought it through: that its caudal fin is horizontal, not vertical as it is on fish. When I mentioned this to my sister she said:

"You're becoming like Aunty Fífa."

Mom says the same, "birds of a feather living up to their name".

In fact, on various and unrelated occasions, she has a habit of saying: "You're named after…"

When I recently made the effort to make a pavlova using one of my grandaunt's handwritten recipes, she said, "You're christened after her."

Eat, drink, sleep, love, communicate, share,
discover and sacrifice oneself for others

Our parents ran and still run a funeral parlour in Bólstaðarhlíð, a small family business, along with my brother-in-law, my sister's husband. The company is doing well, it's *blossoming* as my mother put it, because everyone has to die. My paternal grandfather founded the company and made the coffins himself, quality, reliable caskets out of good wood. Times have changed because now they are *disposable and imported*, as my father put it. There is therefore a long tradition in the family of handling people at their points of entry and exit, as my mother rightly pointed out, on the maternal side when they come into the world and the paternal side when they leave the world; the maternal side when the light comes on and the paternal side when the light goes off. My mother is the exception on the matrilineal side and, at difficult moments, says that she frequently regrets not becoming a midwife like the other women in her family. My sister and I were brought up with my mother going over orders for mortuary cosmetics at the dining table and organizing coffin-closing ceremonies over saucepans. As she was rolling the pieces of haddock in breadcrumbs, she'd say "life is but a match that burns for a brief moment." Or "man is a firefly." If it was a difficult funeral, meaning that the death had been a sudden one or a child had died, she would sometimes lock herself in the bedroom and lie on the bed and refuse to come out. Then our father would tie an apron around himself and boil some sausages. If we could smell hot dogs when we got home from school, we knew that a child had been buried. We would hear our father speaking in hushed tones in the bedroom, talking our mother round.

He would bring her food and we'd hear him say, "if you like we can sell the business." Once she stayed in the room for three days and, when she eventually opened the door and stepped out, she was chirpy and gave my sister and me a long hug and said that it wasn't enough to only have a beating heart. "I want to feel that I'm alive," she said, "to eat, drink, sleep, love, communicate, share, discover and sacrifice myself for others."

I was little more than a pipsqueak when I first took a bus from our neighbourhood down to Hringbraut. I had my own room at Ljósvallagata, which my childless grandaunt always called the children's room, cakes were my daily bread and I was given her undivided attention, unlike at home where I shared a room with my sister and slept on the upper bunk.

"We namesakes," my grandaunt said on various occasions.

We namesakes sat opposite each other at the dining table and played Go Fish. The kitchen cupboards were crammed with cans; she called it her can collection and invited me to choose. I'd point and she'd pick up a can of Ora fish balls and make a pink sauce, then I'd point again and she'd stick the can-opener blade into a can of pears and whip some cream.

Looking back on it, I think I was fleeing the overwhelming and inescapable aura of death that hovered over the house in Bólstaðarhlíð. What if the next child was me or my sister, how many days and nights would my mother then lock herself up under the covers for?

My sister and I worked for the family company during our summer vacations in high school, and part of my job was to wash the hearse, polish it and refill it with gas. I once forgot to fill the tank and the entire procession ground to a halt at the gas station on the way up to the graveyard. On a few occasions, I went along to collect a body in the black van and waited at the wheel, with the engine running. I also remember I once stepped in for Mom and walked in front of the coffin, in a black suit of hers that hung loosely on me, three sizes too big. In a speech she made at my graduation party, she said that every person is forgotten. After three generations we're all forgotten. Eventually only one person remembers you. Is maybe familiar with your name. In the end no one knows you ever lived.

The beginning of a journey
from darkness to light

My shift is over and I shove a box of candy from the engineering couple into my bag. It has a picture of a conical mountain and undulating northern lights on its lid; in fact the whole sky is a spectacular glow of green, pink and purple. I clock out as Vaka, the youngest midwife on the ward, clocks in for the night shift. We met when I instructed her during her internship. Since graduating, she has visited Ljósvallagata several times to seek advice and unburden herself. Interns sometimes cry when a baby is born, even if the birth is normal. They cry with the mother and they cry with the father and they sometimes need comforting.

A woman in labour says I can't take it any more and the intern says the same.

"I can't take it any more."

I tell them "yes, you can take it."

They ask "what if a partner pops out to get something to eat and the baby is born in the meantime? Am I liable for that? What if the partner dozes off during the birth? Should I wake him up?" Freshly qualified midwives might also be afraid of being left alone with a woman in labour for the first time and be scared that they might overlook something.

My young colleague is a member of the Icelandic Search and Rescue Squad and we've sometimes swapped shifts when she is called out. More often than not, it's to search for lost tourists who have gotten their car stuck somewhere or misunderstood inscrutable road signs, people who had intended to take a photograph and driven off track and then lost their bearings because they hadn't realized how rapidly the weather or wind direction could change, that there could be fair weather in the morning but a deadly snowstorm at noon, all changing in the blink of an eye. Or they hadn't taken into account the darkness. There hadn't been many call-outs for tourists this winter, but the SAR team had been summoned several times to help guide stranded whales back out into the open sea. There's been recent talk in the news about the unusually high number of beached whales and carcasses that have washed ashore. This summer the rescue squad had been called out more than once because humpback whales had swum to land. No explanation could be found for the whales' behaviour, but Vaka described to me how her colleagues had sprayed the black carcasses on the beach with water in a race against time to get them back out to sea again. But the next day the whales repeated their performance and swam back ashore.

"The problem was," she said, "that they didn't want to turn around." Not long ago I came across an article that said there were many indicators that the whales' behaviour in the Arctic was changing and that they were no longer swimming south across half the planet in the winter, as they once did. Which might explain the unusual number of stranded whales. According to the article, at first it was the cow whales who had recently calved that were staying behind, but recently males had also been heard singing mating songs by the coast, something they normally only do during mating season when they are trying to woo a partner and the females are fertile.

When the sky is clear, Vaka sometimes takes tourists on northern lights excursions, as a side job. If things are calm on the ward, she looks at pictures of rescue dogs online. She's also compiled a list of the interesting tattoos she's found on the ward's patients, including a cauliflower and a barcoded banana, but also St Peter's Dome in Rome and a farmhouse with a turf roof.

My weekend break is starting, but I'll be on duty over Christmas as in previous years. Even though the hospital tries to give employees with small children a holiday, the fact is that I volunteer. The extra shifts go towards paying the mortgage off on the apartment. There are also plans to renovate the roof and replace the lino on the stairway. Which is why contributions to the condominium fund have temporarily been raised.

I put on my hat and zip my parka up to my throat. This morning a blizzard pelted the roofs of the cars like peas; now a cold shower of sleet splatters my chest. It's difficult to work out which way the wind is blowing. While I'm putting on my mittens, a car drives up and halts right in front of the entrance to the maternity ward. I watch a man hopping out of the driver's seat and running to open the door for a woman on the passenger's side. He supports her as she steps out, and seems anxious; she has a strained expression on her face and a distant air in her eyes, I know the look, a journey from darkness to the light has already started; he holds her arm and, with slow steps, they walk those few metres into the entrance hall. If she is lucky, the baby will be out after a few torturous hours.

The man lets go of the woman to lock the car and grab the case and baby seat, then he has to park the car while she waits in the hall.

I smile at her.

"My waters have broken," she says.

The woman props herself up against the wall by the elevator, droops her head and stares at the lino floor. I think she's about to give birth.

I linger and say "try to breathe."

"My mom had a bad dream last night," says the woman.

I watch the man feeding the parking meter; he reappears with a baby seat in his arms. He's in a state.

"I didn't know how many hours to choose," he says. "I chose six and hope that will do."

The sky has descended on earth and runs through my sister's veins

I hear the phone ring in my parka pocket and have to remove my mittens to answer. It's my sister, the weather woman.

She starts by asking what I'm doing.

"I just finished my shift and am on my way home."

Once she has asked me what I'm doing she normally asks me where I am.

She is also in the habit of ringing off without warning and calling back ten minutes later to add something she forgot and say goodbye again. Phone calls can range between half a minute to half an hour, so I sometimes put her on speaker.

"Are you in the bath?" she once asked me.

She asks me where I am exactly.

"I'm on my way down Barónsstígur."

I could have said that I was at the pathology unit where foetuses and stillborn babies are sent for autopsies. We adhere to standards. A child born after twenty-two weeks of gestation, weighing at least five hundred grams and showing no signs of life, is registered as a stillborn. Otherwise it is registered as a miscarriage.

"How was the shift?"

"Seven babies were born today."

She asks about their sex.

"Four boys and three girls."

I tell her that two sets of them were twins.

My sister is an expert on the behaviour of air masses in the upper atmosphere and, over the past weeks, has warned me about every depression approaching the country, one after another. She tells me a new depression is already halfway across the ocean and is going to wreak havoc. Or that there is another deep vast depression that is just about to strike and will be deeper than last week's. She says we've never seen so many sharp depressions in December before. *Unusual, unnatural* and *unpredictable* are her go-to adjectives when describing *unparalleled* weather. She recently added *unprecedented*. Lately, she has been preoccupied by the depression that she says will hit the country next week. On Christmas Eve or Christmas night at the latest.

"We haven't seen such a dire forecast for this time of the year in seventy years," she now says.

There is one year between us and we are occasionally mistaken for each other; people sometimes say they saw me on the weather forecast on TV and ask whether the brownish clouds are due to volcanic ash east of the desert, traffic pollution from Miklubraut or forest fires overseas? I feel I can hear my grandaunt's voice saying *we all live under the same sky, Dýja dear.* I was once also asked in a queue at the bank whether this winter would ever end, if there was any hope of spring in this country. Then I said, "You have me confused with my sister, the meteorologist." On the other hand, a woman with an infant in a shopping trolley has thanked my sister for delivering her eight-pound son in August.

"That's my sister," my sister then says. And later to me she says, "in a way I'm more like you than myself and you me."

I adjust my scarf around my throat and turn down Sóleyjargata. If it isn't too windy, I walk down Skothúsvegur across the bridge over the Lake, otherwise I trudge along the paths through the Hljómskáli garden, trying to stay sheltered by the trees. If the Lake is frozen, I sometimes shuffle across it.

The connection is bad in the wind and I tell my sister I can't hear her very well. She says she'll call back later.

The last stretch is across the old graveyard, passing the family plot where two midwives are already resting, my great-grandmother and grandaunt. Granny and grand-dad are also lying there and, beside them, a stillborn baby boy who was buried there sixteen years ago. Nowadays stillborns are given names, even foetuses are. I have found four additional midwives in the graveyard and numerous infants' graves. Many of the children were born and died on the same day. From the tombstones I can also usually figure out which women died in childbirth. The mother and child normally share the same date of death.

Christmas lights blink in the windows of nearby houses. The only lighting in the cemetery comes from the battery-powered luminous crosses that are set up before Christmas. I'm at the family plot when my sister calls back.

She wants to know where I am.

I tell her I'm in the cemetery. To be more precise by the rowan tree, which our grandaunt planted.

"Are you going to be buried in the family plot?"

I answer I haven't decided yet.

She wants to know if the tent is still in the yard.

Last week I had walked past a grave where a tent had been raised in a neighbouring plot. It was there for several days and, at first, I thought it might have been pitched by a foreign tourist, but when I took a closer look, I realized it was a beige working tent without a base, like those once used for roadworks. I later discovered—after the issue had been covered in the news—that bones were being disinterred for a paternity case.

It is rare for issues of this kind to immediately crop up in the maternity ward, but I remember one or two cases when a woman was visited by more than one man who wanted to see the baby.

I tell my sister the tent is gone.

Then she wants to know if the leaf is still on the branch.

I had been struck by the sight of a solitary golden leaf on a branch of the rowan tree in mid-December and had mentioned it to my sister. I checked on it daily on my way to work and the leaf hung on by a thread in the wind for days on end. She found it remarkable that a single leaf could withstand such a wind force and wanted me to take a snapshot of it on the phone and send it to her. I tell her the leaf has disappeared, that it probably blew away last night.

Flora Islandica

I stick the key into the lock, open the door and grope for the switch by the coat rack to turn on the light. The fringe chandelier from my grandaunt's estate comes on, then flickers several times, emitting a buzz, like when a fly crashes into a glowing bulb and its transparent wings burn up. Then the light goes off. I've been having difficulties with the electricity in the apartment for some time now, both with lights and sockets, and that's the second bulb to blow in the corridor in the space of a week. I unzip my parka and hang it on a hook, then fumble along the embossed orange vinyl wallpaper, searching for the switch in the living room.

The apartment I inherited half of included its entire contents. Two household inventories as it happens because when Granny died, part of her belongings were moved into the basement of Ljósvallagata and were now stuck there. It was a great relief to my mother not to have to go through two death estates. This explains the lack of harmony in the interior decor and why I have two clashing sofa sets, one covered in burgundy red velvet, the other in dappled grey patterns.

"Like thick banks of fog," my sister says. There have long been plans to give the apartment a makeover and my sister has frequently offered to help sift through the belongings.

"This is like a Red Cross charity outlet. Or a storeroom on top of an antique shop," she says, offering to get my brother-in-law to help out with the transport. Before moving into Ljósvallagata, I'd lived in rented accommodation in various parts of town and my brother-in-law had once moved a bed and a few boxes of books in the back of the glowing black van marked with the funeral company's logo.

I sleep in my grandaunt's teak bed, a small double. In the bedroom there is also a desk where my grandaunt sat, rummaging through various papers after she retired, and two bedside tables as well as a teak chest of drawers. On the floor in one corner of the bedroom, next to the ironing board, stands an old computer which I had encouraged my

51

grandaunt to buy and attempted to teach her how to use. It looks like a small old TV. In the living room there are teak shelves and a sideboard with an old television set and the dining table is also made of teak.

"Teak and plush, plush and teak," my sister says.

On the living room floor there is a carpet with yellow roses and, above the TV, a shelf with two porcelain dogs and, nestled between them, a photograph of us name-sakes together, taken when I graduated from my midwifery studies. I'm in a blue pantsuit and have my arm around my grandaunt, who smiles from ear to ear and reaches up to my shoulders. She has dressed up for the occasion in a black and silver shimmering dress and is wearing a pearl necklace and earrings.

Through the living room and kitchen, there is a view of the graveyard, but the bedroom window faces the back garden with its path and bins. An old double-trunked maple also grows there.

The bottom drawer of the dresser contains my grand-aunt's sewing kit, a box of buttons, knitting needles and three pincushions. The buttons are in a metal box that once held Swiss chocolates. On the lid there is a picture of a high mountain with spruce trees on its slopes, and everything is covered in snow, which reflects a full moon and stars. Another drawer contains her jewellery and the bathroom cabinet her lipstick, powder case and a bottle of perfume. On one side of the wardrobe hang my clothes, on the other side her Sunday-best dresses. I use my grandaunt's tea towels and pressure cooker, and I still have the curtains she sewed and put up in the seventies. The fridge is forty years old but doesn't leak. When I moved in, there was half a packet of cream biscuits in the kitchen cupboard, a packet of dates, cauliflower soup and five unclaimed cans of Del Monte fruit, both pears and peaches.

The apartment bears all the hallmarks of my grandaunt's handiwork. There are embroidered cushions on every seat—my sister counted seventeen—several woven hoops and embroidered tablecloths. The embroideries on the cushions display scenes of natural beauty, such as the Gullfoss and Dettifoss waterfalls, the Almannagjá gorge, the Geysir and the Keilir volcano, and samples of Icelandic flora, *Flora Islandica*, geraniums, dandelions and mountain avens. Visitors' attention, however, is mostly drawn to a tapestry that hangs over the sofa and depicts Mary breastfeeding baby Jesus. Mary is dressed in a red cloak with blue lining and contemplates the infant, who is sitting on her lap on a bottle-green velvet cushion. The child, who is naked apart from a loincloth, has raised his head from the breast and is holding a thumb to his mouth. The breast and the manner in which the mother of God clutches the breast and directs it towards the child is the main feature and central focus of the picture. Judging by his sitting posture, I would guess it is a five-month-old infant. It strikes me that my grandaunt has put more effort into some parts of the image than others, foremost among these being the breast. While other sections of the work seem to have been almost hastily executed, with broad strings of yarn and few colours, such as the two legless angels in each upper corner of the picture, she uses several types of needle stitches and many shades of wool in the breast. Compared to other parts of the picture, which seem flat, the breast stands out; it's three-dimensional, although I wouldn't go so far as to say it's like flesh, as my sister does. My grandaunt seems to have put the most work into the nipple and used several shades of pink for this purpose, interweaving the threads on top of each other in many layers so that the nipple seems to protrude from the picture, like a button or a doorbell in the dark.

As my sister puts it: the breast rules over the living room.

Apart from the embroidery and the orange vinyl wall-paper on one wall of the living room, the whole interior is brownish: the furniture, fittings and curtains: light brown, dark brown, yellow-brown, reddish-brown. The fact is I haven't changed much in the four years since my grandaunt died. Nothing at all, to tell the truth.

When I look around the bedroom, I realize that it looks more like a study with my grandaunt's desk and papers scattered all around. But that hasn't prevented me from having the occasional night guest. Few of them have been preoccupied with the furniture.

Two hearts

I'd taken two lamb hearts out of the freezer yesterday and put them on a plate in the fridge. I don't often eat meat, but hearts are cheap food which my grandaunt sometimes cooked for us. I open the fridge and take the hearts out; the light projects a triangle on the kitchen floor.

I'm rinsing them under the cold tap in the sink when I hear the hall door opening and closing and movement in the corridor. Somebody is on their way up and I sense the person halting on my landing. A moment later I hear shuffling at the door and fumbling with the handle. There is no doubt that someone is trying to push a key into the lock. I screw the tap off and dry my hands. I'm on my way out of the kitchen when there is a knock on the door.

On the landing stands a pale and weary man with a scarf wrapped around his neck, a suitcase beside him. He holds a key in one hand and greets me in English before apologizing for the bother. He says he is searching for an apartment he has rented for Christmas.

The guy upstairs sometimes rents out his apartment to tourists, but rarely lately. He is a bass player in a band and my downstairs neighbour and I negotiated a deal with him not to plug in the amplifier when he is rehearsing at home. I bumped into him a few days ago and he said he was going to visit his mother in Hellissandur over Christmas, but he hadn't mentioned that he'd rented out his flat.

I explain to the stranger that he's got the wrong floor. My grandaunt's name is still on the bell and I notice him peering at it. I've kept it there and just added my name below it.

"This is the third floor," I say, "your flat is in the loft."

He thanks me and apologizes again and says that he has been travelling for thirty-three hours and hasn't slept. And he adds:

"I live at the other end of the planet. Down under."

He looks over my shoulder, into the darkness.

"The light is broken," I explain.

I close the door and go back to slice off the fat and sinews. When that is done, I cut the hearts into slices and roll them in flour. I'm arranging them in the pan when I hear the phone ring. It's still in my parka pocket. It's my sister, I put her on the speaker and place the phone on the draining board while I'm frying the hearts. She asks me what I'm doing and I tell her that I'm cooking.

She asks me if I've got her on the speaker.

I admit I have.

Then she wants to know what I'm having for dinner.

"Hearts," I say.

"And how are you going to cook them?"

"Fried in the pan with onion."

"Do you use oil or butter?"

"Oil."

"Do you roll them in flour?"

"Yes, I do. And salt and pepper."

The frying pan and the flour canister both belonged to my grandaunt. The canister is enamelled, with a picture of a kitten on the front.

I tell her that, when I've finished frying the hearts, I'll add water and allow them to simmer under the lid for a quarter of an hour.

"And what are you going to have with them?"

"Boiled potatoes."

Then she wants to know if the electricity is still wonky. I had told her that I can only use two of the hotplates on the cooker.

"Yes, it still blows."

And I add:

"Another bulb blew in the corridor earlier."

While I finish peeling the potatoes I tell my sister that a foreign tourist just got the floors wrong and knocked on my door.

She asks where he was from and I say that I didn't ask him because he'd been travelling for over thirty hours.

"But he said he's from 'down under'," I say.

She's impressed and guesses Australia.

"Was he alone?"

"Yeah."

"And did you ask him what he was doing in the country?"

"No, I didn't."

"Did you tell him about the weather forecast?"

"No, I forgot."

I turn off the heat under the pan and transfer the hearts to a plate. While I'm washing the pan my sister says she forgot the main issue, i.e. to talk about the planned dinner on Christmas Eve. I tell her I'll be working and that nothing has changed since the meal was last discussed.

"I'll be on the night shift."

"On Christmas Eve?"

"Yes, on Christmas Eve."

"That's when the bad weather will be striking. The explosive cyclogenesis."

At this point I could have said that babies are born regardless of the weather forecast. Whether the sun is high in the sky or low in the sky.

"So you can't eat with us."

"No."

She reminds me that I also missed the Christmas dinner last year and the year before.

"I don't think it's fair," she says, "that just because you don't have your own family, you always have to be on duty at Christmas."

There is a brief silence on the line.

"Mom will be devastated," I hear her say.

At our last family dinner, my mother had spoken about death all evening. Dad nodded and my brother-in-law followed with interest, but as the evening progressed, he disappeared into the kitchen to load the dishwasher, while my parents continued to discuss the price and quality of

58

wholesale coffins and outstanding orders. When Mom had knocked back a shot of port, she said:

"Many would have wanted to add one or two sentences to their lives."

"People die at Christmas just as much as any other time of the year," my father interjected.

Next my sister switches the topic to my Christmas present and whether I've given it any thought. What I want.

"No, I can't think of anything. There's nothing I actually need," I add.

"Mom also needs a suggestion for a gift for you," she says.

Whenever Mom phones she finds it difficult to end the call and the conversation stretches on. The same applies to when we meet and she is saying goodbye; she gives me a long hug and finds it difficult to let go of me and I know that in each case she's thinking that this could be the last time. Apart from her ability to organize funerals, I was brought up knowing that our mother had problems making plans ahead of time. Is it worth it? is a question she often asked. She was surprised when the dentist gave her an appointment in a year's time "what if," she thought; even planning a trip to the theatre could be a conundrum, because one never knew, "what if" she couldn't use the tickets; she had seen two empty seats in the best sections of the middle of the auditorium often enough. Similarly, it was risky to organize a vacation with too much notice, which resulted in her seldom venturing any further than the garden in Bólstaðarhlíð, with a bucket and rubber gloves.

To finalize something was to die, to complete something as well. Life isn't something you hold firmly in your hand, and she is always expecting to be collected, for her turn to come; she's seen too many people depart too soon, it comes with the job. "Every time I walk in front of a coffin," she says, "I think that's not me. Not today. Not this time." "Yet another day without me being collected" was her refrain after every funeral. She is also in the habit of coming for visits unannounced. Then she heads straight into the kitchen and, before I know it, she is standing at the sink washing up, even if there is only one cup and two teaspoons to wash. After that, she dries the draining board. Then she moves into the living room and shakes the cushions. Next she picks up the books lying on the coffee table and puts them back on the shelves. Finally, she sticks a finger into the soil of the plants on the windowsill to see if they need watering.

I inherited a whole forest of potted plants from my grandaunt.

Some of them my grandaunt had received as seeds and cultivated. When I was living with her, she gave herself plenty of time to introduce me to each and every plant and allowed me to touch the leaves to feel their texture. She also pulled a plant book off the shelf and looked for pictures of pot plants in their *natural environments*, on their *home ground* when there was *still weather* all year round.

"All my plants wither," says my mother. "Even the ferns."

I could well believe that I'm the owner of the oldest begonia in the northern hemisphere. I water it twice a week. Under the flower pot there is a fading price tag with the date indicating when my grandaunt bought it. It was forty-eight years ago.

"Unlike mankind, Dýja dear," said my grandaunt, "plants turn towards the light." That was one field of comparison, man and plants, the other field was man and animals.

"Always leave the world the way you would like others to find it when you're no longer around," says my mother.

Gwynvere

One evening, when a year had passed since my grandaunt's death, I decided to go through her jam-packed desk, drawer by drawer. One was locked, but it didn't take long to find the key in another drawer. I seem to remember now that my grandaunt had spoken about a key when I visited her in hospital after she'd had the heart attack. That she might have said that the key to the top drawer is in the bottom drawer. When I turned the key I discovered bundles of letters, an entire collection of letters in fact, bound in a cross of red knitting yarn. All were from the same correspondent,

61

Gwynvere, a midwife in Wales who, it turned out, had been my grandaunt's pen pal for decades.

The collection also contained one letter in my grandmother's handwriting which had obviously been returned because *doesn't live here any more* was written on the envelope. As far as I can make out, the same drawer also contained some rough drafts, which my grandaunt had kept. They show that she'd crossed out words and even whole sentences and made corrections with the help of an Icelandic–English dictionary, before writing out clean copies of the letters. The same drawer also included postcards (in a tin box of Swiss chocolates similar to the one in which the buttons were stored, also depicting high mountains, except that here everything wasn't covered in snow; it was summer and cows were grazing high up the slopes. I was later to discover that the chocolates also came from the pen pal.). The postcards had been sent from many different locations, both from the UK and Europe, and one from America. They all had the same subject matter, more specifically, reproductions of famous paintings of the Virgin Mary, either pregnant or with baby Jesus.

I browse through the postcards. One of them grabs my attention and looks familiar. It depicts Mary breastfeeding a child and I don't have to rack my brain for long to realize that this was the model for the big tapestry in the living room. The back of the card reveals that the work is by Jean Hey, a fifteenth-century Flemish artist, oil on wood.

I notice, however, that my grandaunt has altered a number of details in her version of the picture. She omitted two of the four angels in the background, for example, and simplified most of the stitches, in accordance with the laws of embroidery, with the exception of the breast. I also notice that the Virgin holds her breast differently in my grandaunt's depiction, directing it towards the child, unlike the painting. The embroiderer also allows the child to hook his little fingers around the mother's finger in her work. On the velvet cushion on which the infant is sitting, my grandaunt has woven a flower, which isn't to be found in the original image; a mountain avens, as far as I can make out.

It is clear from their correspondence that the pen pals have discussed the subject matter in the cards because Gwynvere says that she agrees with my grandaunt that the light doesn't shine on the child but rather emanates from it. *It became even clearer when I stood face to face with the original,* writes the pen pal. A few lines below she writes that the original mother of light was probably an adolescent mother, *a girl no more than fourteen or fifteen years old in southern Palestine.* This gives the pen pal an opportunity to spill a considerable amount of ink on *juvenile mothers* and children born *without a father.* *I've been thinking,* Gwynvere writes, *about what you were saying, how it's quite common in your country for children to have children, and the old belief that good luck will shine on children's children. It's a little bit different over here.*

Zoos

My grandaunt corresponded with her pen pal for forty years and, as far as I know, they only met once. That was in 1977, the same year I was born. Mom said that Dad had both dropped off and picked up our grandaunt at the airport and that she hadn't accompanied them herself because he went in the company hearse which could only fit one passenger, apart from the load in the back. That was my aunt's only journey abroad. On her trip she visited a zoo and art museums, but it's quite remarkable that there is no reference to the trip or the meeting of the colleagues to be found in their correspondence.

It was around this time that my grandaunt started to send articles, mainly about the protection of animals but also about how man treated the earth, to various newspapers. My grandaunt carefully kept the clippings of the articles that were published in the papers in a thick folder in the desk drawer, and the folder also included several typed articles which, as far as I know, were never published anywhere. The oldest article, *On the poor treatment of animals in zoos and their natural habitats*, was written shortly after her trip abroad and the most recent about forty years later, just before she died at the age of 93.

I vaguely recollect occasionally seeing newspaper articles with a picture of my grandaunt when I was a kid. They said that the author was a midwife and the same photo was

64

always published with each piece, that of a young woman in a fifties midwife's uniform, a white blouse and white coat, looking up towards the right corner of the picture, with a focused and solemn air. The message in my grandaunt's first article was clear: the animals of the earth needed to be protected from the most dangerous animal of them all—the human beast. *There is no reason to keep predators like hyenas trapped in small cages, just so that man can hold a mirror up to himself* is one of the sentences to be found in it. Given that the word animal had a positive meaning in my grandaunt's mind, her message was not entirely free of paradox. In the article, my grandaunt also spills a lot of ink describing the *deplorable conditions* of a polar bear in the zoo, where the animal is *far too hot*, she says. It is of particular interest to me that she is already referring to a subject which she would go on to write about in numerous other articles, that is, the melting of the world's largest water reservoir, the Arctic ice and glaciers. *If this persists*, she wrote, *polar bears will be extinct within a few decades*. She writes that the world is likely to *run out of water* around the same time.

I cannot help but think that, although scientists had already pointed out the same things and flagged what was going on long before, it was not common forty-three years ago for members of the public to write about polar bears in newspapers.

Browsing through the folder of clippings, it is clear that my grandaunt covered a broad area of subjects. One

65

article talks about the ownership of family pets, saying that animals belong in their natural environment, not in cities where *they get run over,* another one is about the depletion of forests, or to be more precise *man's compulsion to clear and burn forests to create pastures.*

The articles ran in various newspapers, including *Morgunblaðið, Tíminn, Þjóðviljinn* and the *Farmer's Journal,* but it is also clear that not all of them met with the approval of editors, since some only exist in typed draft form. I cannot see any sign of the *My begonias* article having appeared in print, which states, among other things, that these potted plants originate from tropical, fertile soils and warm climates where they grow outdoors. *A characteristic of potted plants is that they can be shifted from one windowsill to another and be transferred when moving between apartments.* The article ends rather abruptly with the following sentence: *Although potted plants need man when they are in pots, other laws apply when they are out in the wild.*

Sperm

My attention is drawn in particular to the draft of an article from 1978, entitled *About sperm.* It opens with the following words: *In my work as a midwife, I have become aware of the growing difficulty couples have conceiving children.* Later my grandaunt writes that she suspects the explanation lies in the emission of toxins and pollution in the seas of the world, which she calls *our shared oceans. I have discovered,* she writes, *that men sail out in ships with their lights turned off to dump hazardous waste and pump toxic materials into the sea under the veil of the night.* In the same article she also claims to know from *reliable sources* that fish in the sea are increasingly feeding on plastic. *Then humans eat the fish.* It strikes me that my grandaunt uses characterizations that did not enter general usage until many years later when she writes *the sperm is lazy and can't be bothered to swim to the egg.* As the articles accumulate and years go by, familiar terms appear in the folder such as the *acidification* and *mass extinction of marine life.*

Of the articles that focus on specific animals, and there are many, the vast majority focus on the bee, *the most important animal on earth.* (One could say that my grandaunt didn't mince her words.) *When bees die out, man will die too* is the heading over one article from 1982. *The bee is more important than man* is the title of another article written thirty years later. In the former article the author suggests that *tired bees should be given two teaspoons of sugar mixed with one teaspoon of water. That will get them back to their hive again.*

As far as I can make out, many of the articles are somehow sequels. In 1977, for example, she lists various species of extinct animals: *Several facts about extinct animals and birds that existed in my childhood but have been lost. We lose some every day,* it says at the end of the article. *Eventually we will lose ourselves.* My grandaunt seemed to update and publish this list every now and then, and, a year before her death in 2015, she wrote her last article, *A million species of animals and plants lost forever as a result of man's greed*, and in it she lists numerous animals, birds, fish and plants that have disappeared. The article is accompanied by a photograph of the Lonesome George tortoise.

In my aunt's mind, there was little doubt about why the world has come to this. *Instead of being humble towards the other living creatures he shares the earth with and its plants, man wants to have everything for himself. He wants to own the fish in the sea, icebergs and freshwater rivers, he wants to own waterfalls, he wants to own islands, he would even like to own the sunset if he could. Possessions make man forget that he dies. When a person finally understands what matters, he has often started to ail and hasn't long to go.*

I've spoken to a journalist who worked at one of the papers that published articles by my grandaunt and remembers her well. He says that in the end she had started resending articles that had been published decades earlier. Or rather similar articles, he added.

"So one could say that she was ahead of her time in some ways and also behind her time in other ways," he said. He also remembered a quarter of a century old article, *Warming earth*, which stated that it wouldn't be long before man felt he was locked inside a boiling tin box and that this would lead to what she called a *displacement of people* between countries. It was the words *boiling tin box* that stuck with him. Other articles were considered too specialized to be deemed appropriate and were therefore not published, such as one titled *Unnecessary*, which discussed how one of the biggest lakes in the world, the Aral Sea, was on the point of disappearing because the rivers that flowed into it were used to *produce cotton clothing for people who already possessed too many unnecessary garments.* The draft, which is to be found in the folder, draws a beautiful picture of the people who previously lived by the lake, and the copious fishing grounds and beautiful sunsets. Then the author of the article assumes a prophetic tone and says that it won't be long before *the lake turns into a desert and long-legged horses are replaced by sandstorms and camels.*

My grandaunt confided to me that, after her trip abroad when she visited a zoo and a museum that exhibited the work of Jean Hey, she made an attempt to *stop eating animals*, as she put it. It had been complicated at that time because of the very poor selection of vegetables in the country. There was nothing but potatoes on offer from September to June, she said, with white shoots sprouting by the end of the winter. The tomatoes and cucumbers from Hveragerði weren't available until the end of June, carrots and turnips at the end of the summer. And the odd head of cauliflower, although mainly if one was lucky enough not to live in a block of apartments and had a patch to cultivate in the garden. She had in fact grown cress herself on the kitchen windowsill. Then it suddenly occurs to me that my grandaunt used to say things out of the blue like: *To think that a tomato only has slightly fewer genes than man.*

69

Uttarakhand

I sit on the velvet sofa with the hearts and turn on the news. Tension is mounting between states in various continents, and armies are gathering on borders, before the focus switches to the imminent storm on Christmas Eve, the sharpest depression ever to hit this country, as the weather expert, my sister's colleague, puts it. Power cuts are expected nationwide and it seems Christmas masses are likely to be cancelled. At the end of the news, there is a small item about the fact that in one hundred and thirty-two villages in the state of Uttarakhand in India not a single girl has been born over the past three months, only boys. I can almost hear my grand-aunt's comment: *They might have problems multiplying themselves.*

After the news, I watch the beginning of an interesting documentary about a reserve for endangered parrots on the island of Puerto Rico. A female parrot that lives in the sanctuary fails to lay a fertile egg. They show her being anesthetized and cut open to examine her ovaries. The experts believe that she possesses maternal instincts and they decide to make her the surrogate mother of another egg. The risk, however, the expert explains, is that she will trample on the egg and destroy it because it is not her own. The documentary also shows that when hurricanes strike the island, the sanctuary's population swells up.

When a woman has been given painkillers or an epidural, she often wants to watch nature films. In my experience

70

David Attenborough's series help many women to relax at birth, even though the undertone might be the extinction of animals and plants and humanity's last days on earth. As one of my patients put it, when she heard Attenborough's voice she felt secure and had no worries about the world. I know everything will be okay, she said. She added that his melodious voice reminded her of her grandfather's; he had been a tinsmith and actually didn't talk much. "When I think about Granddad I can smell metal and oil," she said. As soon as she mentioned her grandfather, she grew emotional, her voice began to crack and she wanted to know whether the moment had come for the baby to be born. When a woman asks whether the moment has come, she is normally halfway there.

Then she took off the headphones, switched off the computer, laboriously tilted her heavy body over to one side, turned her back to me, allowed her legs to slide off the bed until they touched the floor, propped her hands against her lower back, stood up, rummaged through a bag on the chair, found a toothbrush and a tube of toothpaste and vanished into the bathroom. I heard her unscrew the top. When she came back she phoned her mother and I heard her say:

"The midwife says it won't be long before I hold the baby now. If not this evening, tonight at the very latest."

I sometimes peep at the wildlife documentaries on my patients' computers and, not long ago, I discovered that the

71

last white rhinoceros in the world is now extinct. That is to say the male. There are two females left.

I have a feeling the lamp inside the TV is about to give in and I turn it off.

A man is first born naked

When I lived with my grandaunt, on various occasions she would say, *imagine, he was a naked baby once upon a time. Or, and to think she was once a naked infant.* The occasions differed, but the bottom line was always the same: before a man started to persecute those who didn't share his opinions, he came into the world stark naked; before a man made all those wrong decisions, he was fifty centimetres long. But the question wasn't just what had gone wrong, what had happened in the meantime, what had made him capable of committing more atrocities against his own kind, nature and all living things than any other species on earth, but also what it was that made some seek beauty and others not? Just think, she said, as she sat with the album cover on her lap and closed her eyes to surrender to the power of Horowitz playing Franz Liszt's "Consolation No. 3 in D flat major"—and she didn't have to add anything more, I knew what she meant. Or she pulled a poetry book off the shelf and *a quivering tone from a hidden instrument resonated through the living room.* To think that poet once weighed three and a half kilos, I heard her say.

The shelf rails in the living room contain my grand-aunt's library and part of my grandmother's book collection. They both had considerable numbers of volumes of poetry and they sometimes had copies of the same book. I vividly remember the two sisters, Granny and Aunty, on the sofa during family gatherings, both reading a poetry book. In fact, one can even find three copies of certain poetry books on the shelves because ever since I was a child my grandaunt started to give me copies of the books she loved as presents. A few volumes of poetry that had been passed down by the sisters' mother had also found their way there. Most of them were gifts from locals and some are signed: *To my children's midwife.* Some of the books are written by women my great-grandmother knew and were printed in very limited numbers. Then they wrote *from the author* on the flyleaf. Most of the poems are odes to bright spring nights, vegetation and life, but in between there are also some verses written on the occasion of an important anniversary or the death of neighbouring farmers.

Towards the end, my grandaunt was starting to reread the same books over and over again. Her lips moved and she sometimes dabbed an eye after reading, and spoke about the precariousness of life and the light. How scant the light was. Occasionally she read a few lines out loud for me.

I want to see your blood flow
Out into the deep sand.

73

At the end of the reading, she said:

"The beauty, Dýja dear, the beauty."

I don't remember her often quoting patriotic poets, except for two lines from the poem *Iceland* by Bjarni Thorarensen and used on various occasions.

To your ancient womb you should recoil,
Fatherland!—and sink back into the waves.

On the bookshelves one can also find a few biographies and travel books, a book about the interpretation of dreams, and also an art book from my grandaunt's pen pal in Wales, with pictures of the Virgin Mary. Then two shelves are occupied by the entire *Encyclopædia Britannica* and one can still see the many bookmarks and notes which my grandaunt had stuck into the volumes when she was reading up on animals and plants. Finally, two books in particular draw my attention, one a collection of poems by the Argentinian poet Jorge Luis Borges and the other a Danish translation of a book by the French philosopher and mathematician Blaise Pascal. Inside *Tanker* or *Thoughts*, my grandaunt has placed a white crochet bookmark and written her name and the year of the purchase of the book, which shows she was seventy-seven years old when she acquired it. She has also marked one passage with a cross in the margin. I read: *On all sides I behold nothing but infinity, in which I am a mere atom, a mere passing shadow that returns no more.*

Let there be light Ltd.

Then it enters my mind that on a night shift a few weeks ago, I delivered a firstborn who was ten days overdue. When I discharged the mother and child a few hours later, the father handed me a business card and said that if I ever needed an electrician, I shouldn't hesitate to call.

"Any time of the day at all," he said.

It was only fair since I had delivered their baby at two o'clock in the morning, he added and said that he would give me priority.

"Don't hesitate to call," he repeated while he held on to my hand and thanked me for *everything*. The birth had gone well and in my experience the less the midwife does the more gratitude she gets.

It doesn't take me long to find the business card in a kitchen drawer, under the one that contains my grandaunt's teacloths, among matches, tealight candles and batteries. It reads:

Let there be light Ltd.
www.letttherebelight.is

I get my phone and check the time. It's half eight on a Friday evening.

The electrician answers immediately and seems happy to hear my voice when I introduce myself. I can hear the

75

sound of a whinging infant close to the phone and then a voice asking something in the distance. "It's the midwife," I hear him answer.

I ask how the mother and child are faring and he says the child is thriving and I sense he puts a special emphasis on *the child*. He says that, in fact, he's got the little one on his shoulder, that he stays awake at night and gets tummy aches. He then lowers his voice and I get the impression that he wants to add something. Instead he asks what the problem is.

I tell him I've had to frequently change bulbs in the apartment, to be more precise five bulbs over the past two weeks and that the electricity cuts off.

"You haven't been fiddling with the electricity?"

"No."

"Haven't been hammering or drilling near electric cables?"

"No."

"And no youngster with a computer, phone and four devices plugged into the same socket?"

"No, no youngster."

I list off the places where the electricity cuts off and last mention the fast-boil kettle.

"When I plug in the fast-boil kettle the power cuts off in the kitchen."

I tell him the kettle is getting old and that I've wondered if it might be the flex. The same can be said of the cooker, I can only use two hotplates.

He lists a number of possibilities and talks about circuit breakers and fuses. If it's the circuit breaker, the power in the entire apartment would cut off, he explains. Otherwise it's the fuse. If it's neither he might have to look at the cables. Maybe the electricity in the flat was set up by amateurs.

He then asks me for the address and says he happens to live in the neighbourhood.

And what's more, he says he's coming over right away. He's free at the moment, he says.

"You have to be able to plug in your Christmas tree lights," he ends up saying.

I think I hear some movement upstairs from the tourist.

And then there was light

While I'm waiting for the electrician, I tidy the shoes in the corridor. Then I walk right up to the mirror and take off my glasses. One of the things I've been saving up for is laser treatment to fix my short-sightedness. It's difficult to always have to remove my spectacles and wipe them out in the rain and wind. Or a snowstorm. They also steam up when I bend over the women in the birthing pools.

It isn't long before the electrician rings to say he's outside. The intercom isn't working so I dash down to let him in.

"You need a light out here," is the first thing he says to me.

He's holding a toolbox and climbs the stairs two at a time.

When he enters, he gazes around and looks surprised.

"Is this your apartment?"

"Yes."

"And do other people live here?"

"No, I live alone."

"I would have guessed this apartment belongs to a person who is forty years older. It doesn't look like you've been doing much work on it recently."

I show him where the fuse box is and he pulls out a torch to examine it. Then he wanders between rooms, switching lights on and off, tugging at cables and examining connections and sockets.

"You've got hand-painted lampshades, brass rings and copper bulb mounts, textile cables, both simple and interwoven. You don't see many of those these days."

I notice him eyeing the piles of paper on the desk.

"Are you writing?" he asks.

"Those are my grandaunt's," I say. "She lived here before me."

He eyes me up.

"She was also a midwife," I add.

He continues his inspection and says he has never seen an apartment so crammed with furniture and stuff.

"You've got the whole package: a *God bless this home* sign, a bureau desk, porcelain dogs and souvenirs. And two sofas."

He positions himself on the rug with the golden roses in front of the big tapestry over the velvet sofa.

"Is that Mary with baby Jesus?"

"Yes."

"Breastfeeding?"

"Yes."

"And did you sew it?"

"No, my grandaunt did."

"The one who used to live here?"

"Yes."

He turns back to the electricity.

"This apartment needs lighting. You need both ceiling lights and wall lights and you need a spotlight on baby Jesus in the living room. You need a light over the mirror in the corridor and in the bathroom and you need a working light in the kitchen. Personally, I wouldn't fancy handling a knife in this kind of darkness, not even to peel potatoes."

His preliminary diagnosis is that I've been plugging in defective lamps and banjaxed kettles into the sockets and that blows the electricity.

He sticks the torch back into his pocket, but shows no sign of leaving, and instead pulls out a kitchen stool and sits on it.

I sit opposite him at the table and he says it makes a change to get out of the house.

"I'm supposed to be on paternity leave," he says. He grows silent for a moment and then says he has given his wife a sunrise lamp.

79

"A sunrise lamp?"

"It's a lamp that simulates a sunrise," he explains.

He says that an acquaintance of his deals with them and that he can get me one.

"You can get one with an alarm clock and put it on the bedside table in the bedroom."

He nods towards the toaster.

"Or you could have it in the kitchen. Once the socket has been fixed. It depends on where in the apartment you want the sunrise."

A beating hammer from the floor below tells me that my neighbour is either flattening slices of lamb or hanging a picture on the wall. I stand up and pull out a pot to boil some water for the coffee on one of the two hotplates that isn't broken.

I see him stooping and peering at the wall. He is puzzled.

"Is that an Eimskip Shipping Company calendar from 1977?"

"Yes, it's the year I was born," I say.

I can tell he's working out how old I am.

He takes the calendar off the wall and browses through the photos of the fleet of ships:

"Brúarfoss, Goðafoss, Gullfoss, Skógarfoss…" he rattles off. Then he returns it to its place and, while he's at it, knocks on the wall it's hanging on.

At some point my grandaunt had a partition put up between the kitchen and dining room to create a kitchenette.

"Panel," he says. "You could take that wall down and open up into the dining room. Into the living room, actually," he adds, standing up to test the sliding door between the living and dining rooms.

I place the cups and pot of coffee on the table and ask how it's going.

He sits down again, hesitates and finally says:

"Sædís isn't feeling too good."

I say I can give him the name of a colleague in home midwifery services who could offer them some guidance, but he shakes his head and stares down at the tablecloth. It's white with blue flowers embroidered in the corners.

"She can't sleep since she's had the baby."

He strokes the flowers with his fingers.

"She sits by the cradle and watches Ulysses Breki breathe all night."

"It's a lot of strain having a baby," I say.

"I take over in the morning and she makes me swear that I won't let him out of my sight while she lies down."

He continues.

"He had the hiccups last night."

"That's normal."

He finishes his cup and stands up.

"I've been encouraging her to go for walks." He rubs his face in his hands. "Yesterday she wandered out alone into the garden, shovelled some snow and raised her hands to the heavens."

81

He repeats, "she raised her hands to the heavens."

"When she came back in she said, 'Fresh snow and not a drop of blood on it.'"

He shakes his head again. "She speaks in riddles."

I follow him to the door. On the way he tests the switches.

He turns them on and off.

Off and on.

"We're both electricians, me and my brother. Dad is also a master electrician and our sister, who is a kindergarten teacher, is also qualifying as an electrician. So you could say there are four electricians in the family."

"There are also four midwives in my family," I say.

"You could say we work in the same sector then," he says. "Since you're a mother of light, both of us work in light."

He halts by the main entrance and tests the doorbell.

"In fact I've always been scared of the dark."

He repeats that he just doesn't feel good in the dark.

When he is gone I think back to a remark he made at the kitchen table, which struck me as odd. "The best way to make something invisible," he said, "is to lock it in a cupboard."

Father of light

When I moved in with my grandaunt, she had stopped all handiwork and instead spent long hours at the desk in her

82

bedroom with a magnifying glass, rummaging through papers. She had accumulated a wealth of documents, as could be gleaned from the stacks of papers she shuffled and sorted as she jotted down notes. She had an old type-writer, into which she occasionally fed sheets of paper, and could be heard from the living room when she was typing the letters. Mom suspected she was writing her memoirs, which to some extent was true. Her mother, my great-grandmother, who was a midwife up north in *one of the most extensive districts in the country*, had left behind a diary written in small but beautiful handwriting, which my grandaunt had largely typed up by the time I moved in with her. For many years, decades in fact, she had driven around the north of Iceland during her summer holidays with an old tape recorder and interviewed elderly midwives from my great-grandmother's generation. The tape recorder was on the desk and the cassettes were in a pile next to it. I sometimes heard squeaks and buzzes from the bedroom, as I was hunched over my textbooks at the dining room table, while she was listening to the interviews. She had glued brown masking tape on the cassettes and written the name, location and age of each midwife: Blönduós 95 years old…, Hvammstangi 92 years old…, Sauðárkrókur 89 years old…

She had also collected sources on a male midwife, or *light father* as she called him, whom she considered to be a forefather of ours and sometimes spoke about to me. It was

83

more common in some parts of the country, she said, for men to deliver babies, in fact, lines of male midwives had helped women in need over the generations, *from man to man, no less than from woman to woman*, as she put it. Farmers had experience in delivering animals and their own offspring, and then they might deliver babies at neighbouring farms *if they had good hands*. She also knew of a case of a midwife's husband who had stepped in when his wife had just given birth herself and couldn't travel to attend. When I asked her what she intended to do with all this material, she told me that she planned to combine the interviews with the midwives, her mother's diaries and what she had managed to dig up about the male midwife in one book: *Living experiences of seven female midwives and one male midwife in the north-west of the country*.

The true light in straws of grass

It fell upon me to accompany my grandaunt on her last trip up north. Apart from one, all of her interviewees had since departed this world. The youngest, a 96-year-old former midwife, lived on a farm with her foster daughter's son and the idea was to pop in to see her on the way. She also wanted to show me the birthplace of the *father of light*. While my grandaunt still had her full sight and, in fact, even after that, she drove up north on her own every year. The Lada now needed a good jolt to get going and, on the journey, it transpired that there was a hole in the exhaust pipe. When it started to rain over the Holtavörðuheiði moors, I discovered that only one of the windscreen wipers worked. I had completed one year at college when I became my grandaunt's private chauffeur. To everyone's surprise, I had enrolled in theology and it soon became clear on the trip what my grandaunt intended to talk about. As we drove through the Grábrókarhraun lava field, she wanted to know if I was going to become a priest.

I said I wasn't sure.

"Would you be up to burying people?" she asked. "It's not everyone who can write a eulogy," she added, and said that she had heard that priests were also called upon to do a number of things that didn't necessarily fall under their job descriptions. Such as vacuum-cleaning altars, she explained, and shovelling snow off the path for the flock. Parishioners didn't book appointments to discuss which came first, the flesh or the spirit, the spirit or the flesh. I had only taken two introductory courses and done some reading about the Jewish community so I didn't have much to offer. My aunt, on the other hand, was well prepared with scriptural quotations close at hand and it was clear that she intended to discuss the struggle between light and darkness. She said she had loosely counted and concluded that *light* is mentioned in over three hundred passages in the Bible, but that *dark* and *darkness* crop up in about sixty places. She spoke about the light of the world and the light of life and the true light. We drove off the ring road and a gravel track took over, followed by a short stretch of asphalt, which suddenly ended and alternated with more potholes of gravel. We drove past a lake, a cloud rose from the sea and turned into a shower. We overtook a tractor and, a short while later, slowed down to pass a group of horses galloping along yellow puddles, and my grandaunt marvelled at the beauty of the foals before returning to the theme of theology and asking what I thought of the decision to allow God to be born as a speechless child.

We approached our first destination, a farm with a long driveway, which also hosted a church, and there we were welcomed by my grandaunt's interviewee, who came out to greet us and then offered us slices of blood pudding with sugar and mashed potatoes. When my grandaunt inserted the cassette into the tape recorder, I slipped away and sat in the small wooden chapel which had a red corrugated-iron roof and gilded stars on its blue-painted ceiling. When the interview was over, the old colleagues reappeared in the yard, and my grandaunt took a photograph of her friend with an old Pentax camera. As we walked to the car, we were followed by the farmer's dog who sniffed around our legs. Once we were back inside the Lada, I asked my grandaunt what they'd talked about and she answered "midwives having prescient dreams".

The road led over a heath into a narrow, grassy deserted valley, where my grandaunt felt it was right to stop. I supported her for a short stretch from the car, while she scanned the surroundings for what she was looking for. At the centre of a mound, we could just about make out a slightly more elevated tussock in the surrounding peat, which my grandaunt said were ruins. This precise spot, she reckoned, was the birthplace of the male midwife, Gísli Raymond. Overlooking a steep slope, she sat down and I rushed back to grab the camera. On the way, she asked me to also bring her lipstick, which was in the glove compartment. When I opened it, I was confronted by a copy of the Holy Scriptures.

Right as I was taking the picture, the sun broke through and flickered through the straws of grass on the tussock, then a cloud immediately stretched across the sun and the ruins disappeared. I lay down in the heather and when I stood up again my sweater, which my grandaunt had knitted for me for the trip, was covered in mountain aven leaves. When we got back into the car, I asked her what she was doing with a Bible in the glove compartment. Like some travelling preacher. She said she had no idea of how it had ended up in there and assumed it had been left by accident. *By coincidence* were her exact words.

On the drive back she told me that, after some research, with the help of a genealogist, she has discovered that the *father of light* Gísli Raymond Guðrúnarson, known as Nonni, was considered to be of foreign descent, the grandson of a certain Raymond Gísli, who was also called Nonni. It was believed that Raymond's grandmother had once travelled across the sea on a merchant's sailboat and married a priest. It could sometimes be difficult to figure out where my grandaunt's stories were going, because one thing did not necessarily lead to another, on top of which she frequently lost herself in her many digressions. It was often impossible to connect the narrative in any straight line; she spun the thread, but it was as if she somehow always skirted around what was meant to be the real point of her story, until she suddenly cut back to her main train of thought. The genealogist's research stretched abroad and my grandaunt believed she had sources that proved our foremother on the boat was a distant relation, if not a direct descendent, of Pascal, the philosopher who researched vacuums and invented the first calculator.

"I realized how deep our roots stretch back, Dýja dear," she said.

However, she wasn't consistent with herself on whether the male midwife was actually related to us or not, whether his blood ran through our veins. I soon realized, though, that uncertainty and surprise provided the undertone and purpose to my grandaunt's stories, in order to maintain suspense to the very end.

When we drove past Staðarskáli, she finally completed the story, revealing the most crucial element which the entire narrative had been leading to:

"His heart was on the opposite side of his chest."

She had discovered in old documents that the heart of the male midwife in the north-west of Iceland was located on the right side of his chest.

The winding road

Halfway across Holtavörðuheiði, my grandaunt wanted to stop the car to check if there were any berries at the end of July. As soon as I turned on the indicator to pull off to the side of the road, a line of cars prepared to overtake us. She walked a few metres from the car and returned with half a handful of cranberries which she shared with me. As the sun sank, the windows of the farmhouses were set ablaze. Even though it was late at night, my grandaunt wanted to crawl around Hvalfjörður, as we'd done on our way up, rather than go through the recently opened tunnel under the fjord. More specifically, she didn't want to drive one hundred and sixty-five metres below the sea *at fish level*. The still surface of the water mirrored the mountains and sky, as my grandaunt wound down the window to listen to the singing of the birds. The blades of grass on the side of the road stood upright in the stillness.

"Bless you, skua dear," I heard from the passenger seat.

"Bless you, my tern."

She wanted to drive slowly, *to dawdle down the winding road,* as she put it, and that came naturally in the Lada Sport.

Then I got the sudden feeling, as we were trailing past the headland of Hvítanes, me sockless in my yellow sneakers, that I had lived through this before, that we'd had this same conversation before, that I'd heard her say that exact sentence before, precisely in the place where we were at that moment, under the same steep hill:

"Here we are dawdling down a winding road, Dýja dear."

And I knew she would then say that *in every journey there is a new journey.*

Fogbanks hovered over the shores of the Kjós district, and islands and reefs shifted in and out of the mist.

On the way back south I'd had to refill the water radiator twice and shortly after our return, the registration plates were removed from the Lada.

The following autumn I decided to switch from theology to midwifery. My choice surprised my family even more than the theology, everyone except my grandaunt.

"You have the hands for the job, the same hands as your foremothers," she said.

My great-grandmother also mentioned hands in the diary she left behind: *I do my best,* she wrote, *to protect my hands even if it means that people think I don't exert myself enough at the farm.*

Sólheimar—Ljósvallagata

On the bottom bookshelf there are four photo albums. They all have colourful covers, three with floral patterns and one with pictures of puppies. They contain photos of, among other things, my sister and me at different ages in dresses which my grandaunt made for us, but also several snapshots of me alone on different occasions: as an infant in my grandaunt's arms, visiting Ljósvallagata, confirmation pictures, student photos and a shot of me smiling and holding the first baby I delivered. I also recognize pictures that were taken at family do's of us sisters together, and my Granny and grandaunt, side by side, with the same hairdos and hair colour, looking increasingly identical with age. Granny died ten years before her sister, but after she became a widow, it fell upon me to collect the two sisters on the same car trip to family gatherings at Bólstaðarhlíð, collecting one at Sólheimar, the other at Ljósvallagata. They were also taken home on the same car trip. They both lived on the third floors of apartment complexes, and I escorted each of them in turn, two trips in and two trips out; first one of them, holding her arm and helping her out of her coat, then the other. Some of the pictures are of my grandaunt when she was younger. In one of them she is laughing and holding a cigarette in one hand, smoke veiling half of her face. A *woman of the world* were the words a colleague of hers used in the obituary she wrote about a woman who had only travelled abroad once in her lifetime.

One album is crammed with pictures of infants which were sent to my grandaunt inside Christmas cards. The images reflect the parents' varying photographic skills and different qualities of camera, but they are evidence that my grandaunt knitted a garment for every child she delivered. Page after page, I browse through pictures of newborns in knitted garments, making the album look more like a handicraft manual or knitting magazine. Under some of the photos my grandaunt has even written the type of wool and the kinds of stitches used. The back pages contain the photographs I took on our trip up north in the Lada. Most of the shots are of my grandaunt, but one stands out, both because of its subject matter—a dog with erect ears and a curled tail—and the fact that it was taken from a peculiar angle, from above the dog so that it looks like it has no legs. What's more, the picture is blurred. I now remember that I was uptight about the family dog, who made numerous attempts to pounce on me and barked at us when I reversed to turn the car around out of the farmyard of my grandaunt's last interviewee. Under the photo she has written: *Sámur was special in his own way, polite, but not particularly sociable with humans. Blessed be his memory.*

Is there any light to be found in this country?

Soon after we got back south, I suggested to my grandaunt that she buy a computer and offered to teach her how to use it. She was beginning to lose her sight so I showed her how she could enlarge fonts. She was impressed by the ability to correct interviews without having to type them out again from scratch several times. But she frequently needed my help when there was a problem she couldn't handle. Sometimes she said she had pressed a key and the screen had gone black. Or that the document had completely disappeared. But she said it was no big deal, that it was fairly insignificant anyway. No one was going to miss her writing. She sometimes also managed to enlarge the letters so much that there was only one letter per page, beginning with a giant J. On the next page the letter was A, the one after that R with the rest of *Jarþrúðar*'s name, my aunt's interviewee, spread over the following six pages.

In the end I offered to help her type out my great-grandmother's diary and the taped interviews when I was free at weekends. It was then I discovered that *Living experiences of seven female midwives and one male midwife in the north-west of the country* focused very little on midwifery and the delivery of babies, but rather on travelling, the weather and animal life.

In her first diary entry, my great-grandmother explained why she decided to become a midwife. Or, to be more precise, her decision to study at the old Icelandic School of Midwifery. The admission requirements were impeccable morals and complete literacy.

I wanted to travel and see the world, she writes in her fine handwriting, and *I decided to go south to Reykjavík and train to be a midwife. The course took three months. At the same time I took some dancing classes.*

The midwives whom my grandaunt started to interview during her summer holidays, beginning in 1970 and continuing for another quarter of a century, were mostly of my great-grandmother's generation, born between the end of the nineteenth century and the beginning of the twentieth, and shared the common practice of travelling by foot or on horseback to attend to birthing women. *A midwife could say she had seen other horizons*, said one of the interviewees about her vocation.

Most of the accounts described the hardships of travelling in bad winter weather. The midwives were escorted by sturdy young men, who according to their accounts, often gave up due to fear of the dark or exhaustion, so the women would carry on alone, getting lost in blizzards, and having to grope their way, trying to find a familiar rock, sinking into the snow up to their waists, then climbing over or down a mountain pass. They waded across unbridged rivers, trudged over barriers of ice, barely crawled out of avalanches alive, and when they finally arrived at their destination and unwrapped all their shawls, the child was often already born, either dead or alive, *because the weather doesn't always bend to the requirements of a woman in need.*

I typed out page after page about the darkness that had loomed over the island, accounts of bottomless eternal blackness where the midwives couldn't even see their own hands, descriptions of a world of closed walls, sheer cliffs, vertical crags at every step; they try to find the words to evoke what it is like not to see the escort who is standing beside them and having to edge through the night, feeling their way with their fingertips, with no way of knowing what lurked inside the darkness, nor where its perimeters lay, all kinds of sounds— not just the howling of the wind—inhabiting it, sounds they wanted to talk about as little as possible or preferably not at all; the darkness harbours stories, the darkness harbours the imagination and black is black is black. *I've always been scared of the dark,* said one interviewee. In between my grandaunt has interjected some of her own thoughts and interpretations, such as *He who has not travelled around the country by foot in the winter has never experienced true darkness.* And she asks: *Is there any light to be found in this country, is there any light in this world?*

The words which the interviewees used to describe the weather are hardly heard any more, and I sometimes had to pause the tape recorder and rewind to listen again to different terms for blinding blizzards or thick fogs. At the time, my sister was talking a postgraduate degree in meteorology in Lund and I sent her a list of some of the archaic Icelandic weather terms I had come across:

DESCRIBING FOG:

brýla

brækja

dumba

móða

móska

mugga

skodda

sorti

DESCRIBING SNOW:

skari

áfreði

broti

kafaldi

kafaldshjastur

bleytuslag

moldél

kalsanæðingur

snjóbörlingur

kaskahríð

lenjuhríð

blotahríð

fukt

neðanbylur

skafald

skafkafald

drift
fjúkburður
fýlingur
skafbylur
skafhríð
skafmold
skafningur
bleytukafald
klessingur
slyttingur

Even though it was rare, on a few occasions my grandaunt's interviewees encountered beautiful winter weather. It offered hope, as the storm subsided and they saw light in the night sky, *brighter than a sun.*

In January 1922, my great-grandmother, who was heavily pregnant with her eighth child at the time, took on a trip to deliver a baby. On her way home, the weather was still with hard frozen snow and a multitude of stars under a black vault. In her diary entry she writes that the heavens transformed into a ceiling of sparkling mirrors, thousands of tiny mirrors, under a blazing sun. *I slid home over the crust of snow,* she writes, describing crystals that glisten and reflect *the small amount of light a winter day can hold.* It gives her reason to ponder whether man is made of stars. The entry ends with the following sentence: *In the evening I gave birth to a baby girl who lived.*

97

"That was me," my grandaunt interjected when I returned the transcription of the chapter.

Then the summer suddenly arrived, with bright calm nights reported on the tapes. The land changed into green meadows and skipping, gurgling streams. One of my great-grandmother's rather long entries describes a journey with a bag that contained forceps and camphor drops, in a period when time stood still and two months of eternity took over. After a winter of darkness, my great-grandmother finally walks towards the sun, into the shadowless light. *When I looked across the mountain pass, I saw a crack in the clouds as the sun's rays shone down through the nebulous air and my chest under the shawl heaved with joy at the beauty.* She describes the earth as a ravishing green blanket of floss, the hip-high meadowsweet and the mist that comes from a waterfall when she passes by. *I lay on my stomach by the stream, sipped the water, saw a trout, then sat on the bank and watched my reflection slide by, merging with the stream. My mind was as porous as the soil in spring.* She sits on the embankment of a river in a buzz of flies and fills a whole page describing the sunrays breaking into colours on their journey through the water.

I had taken the trout fishing rod with me and a cloud swam in the water. The summer night of the mother of eight ends with the following words: *No one owned me that night and I understood that my life had a purpose.* I turned the page and on the top of the next one she had written in her tidy handwriting: *How can I help people not to have more children? I taught them what*

I knew. The following year I was called back to the farm again to deliver another baby.

Although virtually nothing is said about anything concerning the births themselves and the suffering of the drug-deprived women, isolated sentences can be found in between the descriptions of nature and journeys. *If I had been born a boy, I could have become a doctor and saved the lives of women who died of dysentery*, my great-grandmother writes. On the other hand, both she and her colleagues spoke a great deal about animals. When my great-grandmother talks about her calling, she writes: *As a child I was interested in the birth of animals. It was customary to bury the foetus in the uterus, and I examined the womb of the slaughtered animals and admired the transparent liquid in which the young ones floated. What I found remarkable was that the animals came out with their hind legs first, whereas humans came head first with their arms pressed against their sides.*

Sheep are very prominent in the story.

I enjoy animals, especially Icelandic sheep, says one woman.

Sheep surpass man in so many ways, says another one.

A sheep is man's best travelling companion, says a third.

Icelandic sheep can be stubborn in their own way, says a fourth.

I've discovered though, by comparing my grandaunt's transcriptions of the tapes with what her interviewees actually said, that she not only adjusted questions relating to her field of interest—animals and animal life—but that in some cases she also freely edits and twists the answers. It is, however, clear from my great-grandmother's

99

diary that mother and daughter share the same interest in animals.

In one passage, my great-grandmother mentions a childhood memory of a beached whale and the anticipation when the whale was cut open and the meat was shared. *If luck was on my side they were pregnant cow whales. The climax was when the calf was cut out of the mother. It wasn't eaten.* She also mentions birds. She is on her way for a visit or coming home when she hears a sparrow singing or the golden plover has arrived; she describes the shape of eggs in a nest, she once sees an owl and another time a falcon in flight.

Anything that deviated from the norm also found a place in the accounts of her experiences, such as white ravens and deformed animals. *My greatest interest was in things that were considered abnormal,* my great-grandmother writes. *News of my interest spread across the countryside and they sent for me when joint lambs were born with two heads or five legs.* Accordingly, my grandaunt had considered devoting a chapter of her book *to the abnormal.* If the handwritten note in the margin was anything to go by, for a while she had even entertained the idea of calling the book *Midwives' experiences of abnormalities in the country's nature and animal life.* As the envisaged title suggested, the abnormalities or anomalies applied not only to animals but also to various other natural phenomena. My great-grandmother mentions both lunar and solar eclipses, another midwife refers to a double rainbow, someone else had spotted geese and swans flying together in formation towards the mainland, and believed it was likely that the swans had sneaked into the flock of geese to lighten their flight, another one of the interviewees talked about the strange shape of a cloud, which she describes as the *udders of a cow*.

In the very few instances in which reference was made to an actual birth or baby, it was also in connection with what was unusual or anomalous. There is mention of a baby with *ears protruding at the bottom of the head and a wide gap between the thumb and the other fingers*, and one of the midwives alludes to conjoined twins who'd had a very difficult birth and both died. *But I promised*, she added, *never to talk about the incident.*

I notice that my grandaunt had thought of calling one of the chapters *Maternal instincts.* There, as elsewhere, her personal perspectives are interwoven with the accounts of the midwives. I have come to the conclusion that my grandaunt has always, in fact, been writing about herself, that her interviews with the seven elderly midwives were actually interviews with herself, that their stories were in fact her story, transposed to another time and place, and that the chapter on maternal instincts was no exception. My great-grandmother had ten children, but it strikes me that most of my grandaunt's interviewees were, like her, unmarried and childless. The chapter opens with the words *The purpose of life is not to multiply*, but in addition to a kind of introduction, my grandaunt also includes a conclusion in which she quotes the words of her interviewees. *I haven't come across a maternal instinct in me*, says one midwife and my grandaunt feels it appropriate to add: *Not all women long to be mothers.*

I've actually noticed a pattern in my family of many women having children late. My great-grandmother, for example, was fifty-one years old when she had her tenth child (nine of which were born in May) and, to everyone's surprise, my maternal aunt in Jutland had her first and only child at the age of forty-seven.

When my grandaunt turned ninety, she acquired a laptop and was very impressed when I pointed out to her that she could choose a background for her screen. She hesitated a moment between a sunrise and a sunset against a blazing sky and eventually settled for the sunrise. But even though she'd acquired two computers, she never quite parted ways with the typewriter.

However, *Living experiences of seven female midwives and one male midwife in the north-west of the country* only exists, as an incomplete manuscript, because another work, another idea, soon began to fully occupy her mind and time.

40°C

It's almost eleven and the tourist from the attic flat is standing on the landing in a sweater and apologizes for the disturbance. He is holding a bundle of duvet covers in his arms and says he has been down to the laundry room and is trying to figure out which washing machine belongs to the flat he is renting. It transpires that the boy had freed one shelf and three hangers in the wardrobe, but neglected to change the sheets. The guest says he has been searching for clean bed-clothes, but not found any, and has come to the conclusion that the owner only had two sets, the set that had been left on the bed and another set in the dirty laundry basket.

I slip into my sneakers and, on my way down to the laundry room, he tells me that his son was originally supposed to be coming with him.

"This was meant to be a father and son trip," he says. His son had changed his mind, however, and decided to spend Christmas with his mother instead.

I ask him how old he is and he says sixteen.

"He doesn't want to fly any more. He says the whole of humanity inhales the same air."

He continues. "One day it's winter and the next day it's summer and boiling hot. There used to be a spring for several weeks. Now it only lasts a day. The tulips shoot out of the soil and only live a day. Then it gets too hot."

I show him how the washing machine works. He tells me that initially he had planned to go somewhere else, but decided at the last minute to come here.

"At first I wasn't going to travel this far north, but then I changed my mind," he says.

He doesn't say I've travelled across the entire globe hoping to find a country where everything flows with milk and honey.

He could just as well have stayed in a hotel, he says, but he gave up on that idea and thought it would be more personal to rent a flat. It had been a coincidence that he had ended up in this one because he'd already selected another one, but in the end that owner had decided not to rent it out.

"If you have any whites, put it on eighty degrees," I say, "if you have a mixed wash put it on forty degrees."

He stands beside me and watches as I pour washing powder into the drawer and set the temperature and time. It turns out he has the same brand at home.

I ask him if he's planned how he is going to spend his holiday and he says he's going *to mull things over*. I mull over his choice of words for a moment, *mull things over*.

Then I remember that I did a wash two days ago and have yet to take it out and hang it on the line. I open the machine, take out a T-shirt, give it a shake and hang it up with two pegs. It's inscribed with the name of the bank that sponsored a marathon I participated in to raise money for oxygen saturation meters for newborns in the recovery unit. I pull out a few more tops but hesitate when it comes to my underwear.

As we walk back upstairs together, I offer to lend him some bedclothes.

He smiles with gratitude and lingers on the landing while I shoot into the apartment to get a set of white damask duvet covers decorated with crocheted insets by my grandaunt.

I'm unable to resist asking him if he was present at his son's birth.

He says he was.

I ask him if he was afraid and he says:

"Yes, I was afraid."

I ask him if he cried and he says he cried.

I tell him that whales use midwives, like humans.

"I see," he says.

It's difficult to know what is going through his head. He seems to be thinking it over.

Then he asks me if I'm a whale expert.

I tell him I'm a midwife.

"And how many babies have you delivered?"

I don't have to think about it, I did a count yesterday.

"On Friday I delivered the 1922th child."

Nothing has changed

I pull Mary Seacole's biography from 1857 off the shelf, *The Wonderful Adventures of Mrs Seacole in Many Lands*, and take it to bed with me.

I spend a lot of time with my patients and, if the delivery is progressing slowly, I sometimes grab a book. More often than not it's a poetry collection. If a woman asks me what I'm reading, I lift the book and show her. On some occasions a woman has asked me to read aloud and I do. I was once

105

summoned by my supervisor, who had been informed by a husband that I'd read out a poem about suffering and the loss of a son to his wife.

"That might have been Anna Akhmatova," I said. "She lost her son in Stalin's purges. Many women feel it's good to know that they aren't the only ones suffering," I add. Now that I think about it, I remember one woman who specifically asked me to read a poem about death to her. As a precaution I asked:

"Are you sure?"

"Absolutely sure," she answered.

And I read:

> *Death is nothing at all.*
> *It does not count.*
> *I have only slipped away into the next room.*

It now occurs to me that I could have told the human resources manager that the core of most poems is solitude and the meaninglessness of life. I think back to my grand-aunt's words as she stood by the window with a cup of coffee and said *man enters the world naked and searches for a purpose.*

I put the book down on the bedside table, pull the flex and turn off the light. The beaded fringe of the lampshade quivers.

Now the darkness can come.

And then, once again, light.

II

Zoology for Beginners

"They give birth astride of a grave, the light gleams in an instant, then it's night once more."

SAMUEL BECKETT

Getting used to the light is the most difficult

I peer out in search of a streak of daylight through the window. It's still pitch dark.

I drop some bread into the toaster and turn on the radio, land in the middle of an interview and hear a man explaining that a black hole is a region that swallows all light and devours all matter and nothing can escape it. The situation inside these holes is so alien to us that all accepted ideas of science fail, I hear him say. Even time and space cease to exist in the forms that we know.

I finish the cup of coffee and turn off the radio.

At the bottom of the wardrobe where my grandaunt's dresses hang, she left behind a heavy cardboard box marked with the Chiquita banana logo. I knew it contained papers, but for a long time put off opening it. When I visited her in hospital on one of the last occasions, she patted me on the back of the hand and said:

"You take care of the box for me."

I didn't know what she meant.

I didn't open it until a year after she died.

At the top of it lay a light brown envelope which, upon closer examination, contained a manuscript of over two hundred typed pages. On the front page was my grandaunt's name and below it in capital letters, *ANIMAL LIFE*, subheading: *Investigation into what the human species is capable of.* I skimmed through the pile and it was quite clearly the manuscript for a book. The work began with a preface in which my grandaunt introduced herself as the author: *I have delivered babies on the shortest day of the year and the longest day of the year, when the sun is low in the sky and high in the sky, a total of 5077 babies, 2666 boys and 2411 girls. I have knitted garments for all of them; bonnets or cardigans, but also leggings and pants. Most of them in yellow and light green, the colour of the sun and sprouting plants. I calculate three to four balls of wool per child.*

The preface concludes with the following words: *It is said that humans never recover from being born, that the most challenging experience in life is coming into the world and that the most difficult thing is to get used to the light.*

I soon came to realize, as I dug deeper into the box, that there wasn't just one manuscript but another two. I noticed that all of them are typed. As in the case of *ANIMAL LIFE*, my grandaunt's name appears on the front pages with the titles underneath: *THE TRUTH ABOUT LIGHT* (in the margin she had written two other titles, *My Thoughts on Light* and *My Memories of Light*, as if she had been considering them too) and *COINCIDENCE*. A new preface accompanied each manuscript, and I initially assumed they were three different books. But as I browsed through the pages, I came to realize that all the manuscripts contained the same topics, despite all being strangely different. I started to wonder whether they were all different drafts or versions of the same book. "You'll stitch my work together," my grandaunt Fífa had said. I'd thought she meant in my work as a midwife. Now I'm no longer sure.

Everything connects

I've tried to tackle the box, but it's taken a lot of time to plough through a total of over seven hundred typed pages.

My sister has been monitoring my progress from the sidelines. She refers to the papers as "the stuff" and every now and then asks "have you been through the stuff? Do you want me to help you with sorting and throwing it away?" Or she says, "are you still sifting through the pile?" And adds "you could take that to the manuscript department of the National Library and let them lock it up for fifty years, and the matter will be closed."

When she first asked me what the manuscripts were about, I struggled to answer.

"I don't know," was the first response I gave her.

"Have you no idea?"

"It's difficult to describe it exactly," I said. "It's unlike anything I've ever read."

"Are they memoirs? Like the midwives book?"

111

"No, actually," I said. "The content also varies a lot from one manuscript to the next," I added.

I give it some thought.

"I think she is trying to understand humans," I said to my sister.

"Understand how?"

"Humanity's helplessness."

"Doesn't she trust them?"

"It's difficult to say."

"I see."

"I haven't been through it all yet," I end up saying.

One of the things that has puzzled me the most is the style, or rather, lack of style, because not only are there considerable differences between the various manuscripts, but also from one chapter to the next, and even within each chapter, giving the impression that there could have been many authors. Some sections adopt a dry, concise and scholarly tone, while others strike a more pompous, solemn and even biblical register. One can also find staged dialogues in the spirit of the Enlightenment writings of the eighteenth century. My grandaunt doesn't strive to establish any logical continuity or climax in the structure of her narrative, to ensure one thing necessarily follows another. Matters aren't made any easier by how fragmented the text is in places, as if bridges are missing between the topics. Incoherence or disjointedness were, in fact, the first terms to spring to my mind. Form and content seemed to merge into one, as my grandaunt writes: *One thing does not necessarily lead to another. That is because the world is scattered and man sees only a fraction of a fraction.* Chapter headings also didn't necessarily provide an accurate idea of their content, quite the opposite in fact. They could also be hazy and vague, like the chapter titled *What I know* or the longest chapter in *Coincidence* called *Other.*

The manuscripts also contain a number of disparate topics, isolated sentences and snippets of text that seem to have no contextual relationship with the rest. When I think about it, there are many surprising similarities between my aunt's style and her own mannerisms, particularly her oblique way of talking about things. She also had a habit of saying things out of the blue like "first light and then darkness, first day and then night, that's the order of things." Or "in the centre is where we stand at any given moment, Dýja dear." Or she said, "you will see that men say yes, but mean no. Or vice versa, say no and mean yes." All of a sudden I recall her talking about a black hole in the middle of space. And in the middle of the hole, light. I didn't take in everything she said. Not then. Not when I lived with her. I sometimes got the feeling that what she said was the final conclusion or culmination of something she had been pondering on for a long time, akin to the result of a lengthy mathematical equation.

Most striking of all, though, was how she managed to somehow glide from the microcosmic to the macrocosmic

113

within the space of the same paragraph, from a leaf or knitting stitch to remarks about there being millions of light years between stars in the same constellation. It was as if my grandaunt had been unable to distinguish between what is small and large, between a main issue and a detail. Or rather everything small in her mind was big and big, small. This was consistent with her firm belief that ultimately everything is connected. *In the end,* she writes in *Coincidence, one sees that everything connects.* It therefore matters little whether the structure was like entwined roots or a subterranean maze with secret tangential trails, since at the end of the day they blended together because *everything is connected.* (I can't help thinking that coincidence is precisely the term which best describes the structure and organization of material in my grandaunt's manuscripts.) A loose count indicates that the two words *everything connects* crop up in three hundred places in the manuscripts in various contexts. Whenever my grandaunt reaches a dead end, she writes *everything connects*; that was her way of developing an argument instead of a method of reasoning, and it was also her conclusion instead of a conclusion, *everything is connected.* When I told her I'd given up theology and intended to become a midwife, she said:

"Ultimately one understands that everything is connected, Dýja dear."

Chiquita

When my sister first asked me what I intended to do with the manuscripts, I said I didn't know.

Everything seemed to indicate, though, that our grandaunt wanted to get her writings published. Confirmation of this was found in the Chiquita box in a letter from a publisher in which he thanks my grandaunt so much for sending in a manuscript. He then writes: *We certainly find this manuscript unusual, but unfortunately the material is too disjointed to consider publication.*

The letter is dated October 1988, but it is impossible to determine the manuscript to which it pertains. I suspect, though, that the publisher is referring to *Animal Life, Investigation into what the human species is capable of.* The letter is friendly and it is clear that its author has put considerable effort into the rejection of the manuscript. He apologizes for how long it has taken to reply and says the manuscript got *buried* under a pile of submissions and then that their reader had been off on maternity leave. From the letter it can also be deduced that my grandaunt had visited the publishing house because the editor thanks her for popping by. Finally, he mentions that they've had to halt the planned publication of several books because of the troubles facing the publishing world. The author of the letter treats my grandaunt with tact, I imagine because of her age, but reading between the lines, one gets the impression that he has problems understanding what the manuscript is really about. I sense that instead of the adjective *unusual*, what he meant was *unpredictable* or even *illogical*. On the back of the publisher's letter, my grand-aunt has written her own comment in blue ballpoint pen: *Dissatisfied with the structure.*

My neighbour from the floor below works as an editor for a small publishing house and I once mentioned the manuscripts to her. I was coming home from a night shift, it was a Sunday morning, and she had gone outside to plough the path and brush the snow off the dustbins in the dark; a blue glow from a television indicated that her children were watching some kids' programme.

I mentioned that the manuscripts were slightly disjointed, but she felt that people were more open to fragmentation or disorder nowadays than thirty years ago, and that it could even have the appeal of *bad taste* as she put it. What's more, a good editor could perform miracles by building bridges between disparate topics and finding what she called the *backbone* of the work.

"Then it'll have subject matter," she added.

A small publishing house, such as the one she works for, wouldn't have the means to publish such an unconventional work, but she suggested I speak to other publishers. I should, however, prepare myself to have to explain the purpose of the work.

The question was also which manuscript I should submit.

One possibility was to send all of them in and allow the editor to pick out the best nuggets.

Man is a biped and a mammal

Apart from the letter my grandaunt received from the publisher, which is too vaguely worded to be able to determine the manuscript to which it refers, I don't really have any dates to establish the chronology of the manuscripts. My guess is that they were written over a long period of time, possibly until she died in 2015. The most integral manuscript is *Animal Life* and I think there are indications that it is also the oldest. My grandaunt calls the longest chapter in the manuscript *Man is a biped and a mammal*, but from a scribbled note in the margin, it can be deduced that she had also considered the title: *What do other animals have that man does not?* As the title suggests, the chapter focuses on man as a mammal and how he compares to other animals, and starts with the following sentence: *Man develops more slowly than other animals on the planet.* My aunt's conclusion is that in most regards man lags way behind other animals, not least when it comes to the slow development of their offspring. When I tell my sister that the term most frequently used by my grandaunt to describe humans is mammal, she says that shouldn't come as a surprise, considering our grandaunt's area of expertise. Apart from that, the chapter focuses on

117

animals' abilities compared to those of humankind. *Lambs and foals scramble to their feet at birth,* my grandaunt writes, *but it generally takes a human child up to twelve months to acquire the ability to take three steps, with wobbly legs. It takes a human child two years to acquire a vocabulary of fifteen words,* she continues. *In that time, a female cat has given birth to at least one litter. Much later, a human learns words like footstalk and later terms like cause, freedom and regret, but there is no guarantee he will ever reflect on their meaning.*

Bees and spiders engage in intricate dances and flies dance, my grandaunt continues, *but it takes humans two years to learn how to stand on one foot and jump up and down. Or the same amount of time it takes a human to develop the ability to blow into a harmonica by inhaling and exhaling.* I'm struck by one sentence towards the end of the chapter, not least because it seems at odds with the other material in the chapter: *Like man, bonobo monkeys have reconciliation sex.*

More fragile than a porcelain vase,
than a bird's egg, the most
fragile of the fragile on this earth

Even though humans have *adequate eyesight*, as my grandaunt puts it, she lists various other animals that have far superior and more sophisticated vision, such as eagles, for example, who have a built-in zoom in their eyes and can spot a prey at distances of many kilometres. The best vision of all animals on earth, however, belongs to a particular species of lobster (in one sentence she speaks of lobster but in the next, a species of crab). Her sentences frequently start off by stating human limitations, such as the fact that they are blind in the dark. This is followed by a list of animals who are not blind in the dark but have good vision, and she mentions as examples both owls up in the sky and sharks down in the depths of the sea. After eyesight, my grandaunt turns her attention to hearing and says that even *earless insects* hear better than humans. The senses are tackled one after another, the sense of smell is also weaker in humans than in most other species, and Icelandic sheepdogs are mentioned as an example of an animal that is far more advanced in this regard. *Man is constantly drinking coffee and throwing away water, but a camel can survive in the desert for many days without water*, my grandaunt writes. As for the sense of orientation, *a man can find his way out to a store, but an Arctic tern, that magnificent creature of the skies, can glide between the two poles on its thin wings, masterpieces of nature.* An elephant's trunk can detect movement fifteen kilometres away and the biggest mammal on earth, the whale, can detect the movement of submarines at distances of dozens of kilometres and disrupt their telecommunications equipment. *In fact man should spend his life marvelling at these wonderful creatures.* My aunt's belief that humans lag behind other animals grows with each page. Her conclusion on the biped and mammal is that a newborn baby *is actually as delicate as the wings of a fly, if the small bundle*

119

slips out of the arms of a highly strung (and in some cases smelling of alcohol) father, the light goes out in an instant. I have come to the conclusion that the one who calls himself the master of all creatures is in fact the most vulnerable of all animals, the most fragile species, more fragile than a porcelain vase, than a bird's egg, the most fragile of the fragile on the planet.

A letter from my grandaunt to her Welsh pen pal strikes a similar note when she writes:

The most sensitive creature on earth never actually recovers from being born.

The brain

The second part of the *Man is a biped and a mammal* chapter in *Animal Life* talks about the size of the human brain and the hotchpotch it contains. *Man has a brain that is five times bigger than it should be, considering the size of his body*, my grandaunt writes. *The size of the brain causes humans to worry about tomorrow and not being loved. To be lonely. To be misunderstood.* In this regard, it is interesting to note that, despite the obvious superiority of other animals over man, my grandaunt considers human weaknesses to also be their strengths. *The size of the brain allows man to harbour many thoughts. He can solve problems if he chooses.* A chapter devoted to human limitations begins with the words *Because man cannot fly on his own wings, he builds airplanes.* Similarly, *man's shortcomings*

120

have driven humans to invent electricity and vaccines, clothes irons and computers (she added *computer* to the text with a ballpoint pen after she acquired one herself). The most positive characteristic of humans, in my grandaunt's opinion, however, is how unpredictable their behaviour is, which means that we, unlike other animal species, can surprise ourselves. She describes how people can start to hop on one leg without warning, or stand on their hands without any obvious purpose. *The strangest thing of all is that very often a man doesn't know why he is doing what he is doing. He is a rebel and a maverick.*

It comes as no surprise that, in my aunt's opinion, the most significant characteristic of humans is their ability to write poems. To be more precise, that a man can say that he is *a fish in a net of words and that our words are nets to catch the wind.* And more again: *and your blood flows blind and heavy and impatient.*

The manuscript even contains four pages of quoted poetry, both complete poems and individual lines, which my grandaunt likes. *I will come back to language,* she writes at the end of the chapter, but it is typical of her unreliability as an author that she doesn't. She never mentions language again.

As far as feelings are concerned, my grandaunt considers that humans still live in a cave:

But when it comes to feelings man is helpless and only has a loin-cloth to hide behind. Or even less, he is as naked as he was at birth. He doesn't understand why he feels the way he feels.

You shall

My sister has asked me if births aren't discussed in the manuscripts. I say they're not, apart from a line that says *man is born and dies*. In this regard, like my grandaunt on the midwifery profession, she vows not to put a single word on paper about the births themselves. *No one remembers their own birth and no one has yet managed to put the personal experience of dying into words*, she writes. *Many, on the other hand, have expressed themselves at length about the deaths of others. That's because they dread their own.*

From the correspondence between the pen pals, one can extrapolate some of the things my grandaunt was grappling with, and they discuss mortality in many letters. They write about death scenes in literature and, from my aunt's contributions, it can be gleaned that marriages are, among other things, the cause of the death of characters in Icelandic sagas. On the other hand, the Welsh pen pal spends a considerable amount of time pondering on the death of Lavinia in *Titus Andronicus*, Anna in *Anna Karenina* and Alyona Ivanovna in *Crime and Punishment*.

The chapter titled *Some words of advice to the children I have delivered*, which is to be found at the end of *Animal Life*, reinforces the rumours that my grandaunt had addressed speeches to newborns in the maternity ward.

The speech starts with the words: *Welcome, little child. You are the first and last you in the world,* and it consists of a list

of twenty-nine things that await the child. Each sentence
starts with *You shall...*

1. *You shall share the world with the other animals that roam
   the earth, the birds of the sky and fish of the sea, trees and
   mountains.*
2. *You shall feel a strange longing to accumulate objects and acquire
   things you have no need for.*
3. *You shall see that things will turn out to be different to what
   you expected, that they are determined by coincidences.*
4. *You shall suspect your neighbour and fear he is trying to under-
   mine you.*

"Didn't our grandaunt write anything about fears, longings
and desires?" my sister once asked.

"No, not directly," I answered.

The final sentence addressed to the children of light has
puzzled me and is, in fact, one of the few segments in my
aunt's material which refers to emotional issues.

29. *You shall feel rejection and heartache as if you had a burning
    bush in your chest and you shall have difficulties swallowing.*

I have searched for evidence of her love life in Ljósvallagata
but found little. But when I was going through the bookshelves, I found a handwritten sheet that had been slipped
between the pages of *Flora Islandica*. There were two

123

sentences on the sheet, written side by side, each rewritten a total of seven times.

> *I will wait for you.*
> *I will not wait for you.*

As if she were trying to evaluate the sentences side by side and to decide on which one to choose. I've asked Mom and she said she doesn't know anything. The precise words Mom used were *people don't say anything in the circles I mix in.*

I have also mentioned the twenty-ninth item to my sister and that gave her an opportunity to talk about her husband.

"Things happen that you don't expect," she said.

"Like what?" I asked.

"Sigurbjartur."

"What about him?"

"We had a long conversation yesterday."

She'd recently told me that my brother-in-law was a changed man.

"I suspect he has an admirer at work and that he has noticed and feels flattered."

"You'll realize, Dýja dear," my grandaunt had once said to me, "that what doesn't happen is no less important than what does happen."

The more I try to piece the jigsaw of my grandaunt's life together the more questions it raises.

The world is still black

I wake up on the shortest day of the year into the longest night of time.

It will be a long time before the light dissolves the night and the world takes on a form. I listen out for sounds in the house and think I hear movement in the loft. I get up and pull the curtains back. A soft grey haze hovers over the graveyard. An airplane emerges from a cloud and vanishes into another. The day never really manages to break through.

I'm on my way into the kitchen when I hear someone running up the stairs and, a moment later, a knock on my door. Vaka, my colleague, is standing on the landing and says she slipped in with the man who was on his way up to the loft. She hands me a bag from the bakery, shifts two cushions and settles on the edge of the velvet sofa. When she came on her first visit, it was obvious that the apartment had taken her by surprise. That was exactly what she said:

"The apartment is surprising."

Now she has a serious air and reveals that last night she delivered a baby that was three months before its time.

"She was born too early," she said.

Sometimes babies make you wait and come a few weeks late, sometimes they're born too early, tiny beings with toes the size of beans and a blue web of veins that branch out under their white skin, ever so thin, like rice paper.

125

"She wasn't ready," she says, propping a cushion under her head and leaning back.

"I'll make some coffee," I say and pour some water into the pot and turn on the heat.

It sometimes happens that a baby is born and dies in the same minute, sometimes the heart beats a few times, then the beat fades and the light goes out.

I lay the cups and saucers on the table and butter the buns she brought.

"Did the baby survive?" I ask.

"Yes, she was moved into the recovery room."

My colleague lifts up one of the cups, turns it over and her lips move. Then she says:

"This is the white set from Hjörtur Nielsen's collection."

She is silent a moment while she eats the bun. Then she adds: "I heard you lost a child at birth."

"Yes, that's right. A boy."

"How long ago was that?"

"Sixteen years. In July," I add.

"Was he mature?"

"Yes."

My patients sometimes ask me if I have children and I say no.

Had they asked *have you ever given birth to a child?* I would have answered I almost became a mother.

She sips from the cup, brushes the breadcrumbs off the table and sweeps them onto the plate:

"I had a strange dream last night."

She hesitates and then adds:

"I dreamt I was put in charge of six infants, all girls, and that I was alone with them. I was supposed to feed them, but there was only one baby feeding chair at the table."

Comparisons of dreams on the ward show that it is common for midwives to dream of births in which they themselves are in distress. Also that they dream of infants. My grandaunt could readily interpret dreams. Dreams of having a baby meant great happiness for married women, but difficulties for unmarried ones, seeing a child fall heralded discomfort, seeing a child squabble was a sign of good luck, seeing a child cry boded good health, seeing a child run augured bad things, a walking child signified freedom and many children great happiness. Helpless children, on the other hand, were a sign of problems to come.

"It could mean that you find the responsibility overwhelming," I say.

I also think of the strain of her rescue teamwork. Once she was on a search for a whole weekend and, when she showed up for work on Monday morning, she said that, when the storm blew over, the tourist was found near a hillock where he had sought shelter from the weather.

"We knew we weren't searching for a living man," she added.

I pour coffee into the cups.

"I tell women to listen to their bodies like we're taught. But does the body listen to the women?" she asks and takes

127

a deep breath before answering the question herself: "No, it doesn't."

She sips from the cup.

"It so happens," she continues, "that I've recently looked up how many women die in childbirth every day."

"You mean in total?" I ask.

"Yes, in total."

She looks down.

"Eight hundred and thirty women a day," I hear her say.

She looks up and stares at me.

"That's the equivalent of four passenger jet crashes a day."

She hesitates again.

"It would be on the news," she finally says.

"Yes," I say, "it would be on the news."

She stands up, walks over to the window and stands there for some time.

Clouds grow close then distant, rapidly passing.

The fog finally rises from the cemetery and a blue streak appears at the bottom of the sky and gradually widens, revealing a line of snow-topped mountains on the horizon.

It then occurs to me that she has just moved into an apartment which she rents with her friend from the rescue squad and had mentioned that they need furniture.

I cut straight to the point.

"Didn't you say you needed a sofa?"

She turns around.

"I'm thinking of getting rid of some stuff," I say.

She looks around and confirms she needs a sofa.

"Do you need more furniture?"

When she had come for her first visit she'd walked around the apartment and admired the teak and she now takes another round.

"Are you sure?"

"Yes, absolutely. Take what you want," I add.

She clears her throat.

"Tell me what you can lose."

In the end she chooses the sofa, which my sister likens to a rain-filled heavy winter sky, my grandparents' double bed, which had been taken apart and stored in a room off the living room (the mattress was thrown away) and a dining room set, which also belonged to my grandmother. After some encouragement from me, she adds an armchair and a coffee table.

She makes two phone calls and says she can borrow a trailer from the rescue squad and that two girlfriends of hers from the team are going to help her move the furniture later in the day. First she's going to pop home for a rest.

Eggs

My sister is on the phone.

"Did the electrician come?"

"Yes."

"And what did he say?"

"He said I was plugging faulty appliances into the wall and that the whole apartment needs lighting. That it was like walking into the home of an old blind woman."

That reminds me of the Christmas gifts.

"You could give me a lamp," I say.

She is pleased with the tip and wants to know what kind of lamp.

"A floor lamp or table lamp?"

"It can be either a floor or table lamp."

"You don't need two lamps?" she asks.

"Yes, could well be."

She says she'll let Mom know.

"Haven't you thought about making some changes? A makeover?"

I tell her that, as it happens, I've just given away one of the sofas and some furniture.

"To Vaka, who works with me," I add.

"The one in the rescue squad?"

"Yeah."

She feels this is great news.

Next she turns the conversation to the tourist and asks whether I've found out where he is from.

"From Australia just like you guessed."

"Is he escaping the heat?"

"He didn't mention that. I taught him how to use the washing machine. He said he's mulling things over," I add.

She finds it amazing that a man needs to fly seventeen thousand kilometres to "mull things over".

"Did he explain that any further?"

"No."

There is a lengthy silence on the phone.

Next she wants to know if I need eggs.

"No, I still have almost the whole tray you brought last week."

My sister has a friend who breeds chickens and supplies her with eggs. She regularly brings me some, by the carton load.

"Did you tell the tourist about the forecast?"

"No, I forgot."

The weather forecast has worsened since yesterday. Instead of it being the deepest depression to strike Iceland in seventy years, it's been upgraded to the deepest depression in a hundred years. The main unknown factor now is exactly when the storm will strike. Whether it will be on Christmas Eve or the morning of Christmas Day and at what time of the night.

"Isn't it likely that the Christmas do will be postponed then?" I ask. "Since the forecast is so bad?"

"Yes, we might have to postpone the dinner by a day and get together on the evening of Christmas Day instead." She wants to discuss that possibility.

"The weather should have subsided by then," she says.

"I'm taking three night shifts in a row so unfortunately I can't come," I say.

"The last depression was a picnic compared to what's coming our way after the weekend," my sister ends up saying. That depression had broken windows and blown away a sheep shed under the mountain glacier of Eyjafjallajökull. My sister had also been surprised by how many people still had their trampolines outside in December.

Darkness makes the world invisible

I knock on the door of the loft flat and the tourist greets me in his shorts.

"I just wanted to let you know," I say, "that the weather forecast is not good. They're expecting very bad weather after the weekend."

His shirt is buttoned up wrong. It's one button off. Like a child who has dressed by himself.

"Very windy," I add to increase the emphasis.

"Worse than yesterday?" he asks, "Windier?"

I give this some thought. There was nothing wrong with the weather yesterday. Northern breeze and snowdrift. Best weather to be submerged in a hot tub at the pool. Bodies floating in puffs of steam.

"It's going to be shocking weather," I say and give a brief summary of the forecast.

That reminds me that there is a small balcony off the loft with a barbecue, which the boy sometimes uses to grill

132

lamb chops that send smoke into the neighbouring windows, the last time just a few days ago. I wonder whether I should mention to the tourist that people have been asked to secure loose objects in gardens and on balconies.

Instead I tell him that the weather is expected to worsen at first but that it normally should improve after that.

"So the weather doesn't look good for outdoor activities," I conclude.

But there are still three and a half days until the storm strikes and in the meanwhile the tourist can explore and do various things. That is precisely what he has in mind because he dashes in to fetch a map which he unfolds and spreads out.

He points at several places and says he has been wondering whether he should visit them. Whether I think it's worth it.

I think about it.

"The main problem is how short the days are," I say.

I put it slightly differently, saying that the sun appears over the horizon just before noon but then vanishes again at around three. That the sun struggles to rise every morning and that, three hours after it has finally risen, it starts to darken and the sun sinks back into the ocean again.

I finally summarize the information as follows:

"You'd only have a few hours to see the things you were going to see."

When I'm back downstairs again, I suddenly remember that when the electrician was saying goodbye on his way down the stairs, he made a remark that struck me as odd: "Nobody knows exactly what light is. It's possible to measure it, but not to understand it."

Is it an empire, this light that is going out, or a firefly's glow?

In a thirty-year-old letter, my grandaunt explains to her pen pal that she is working on some kind of *investigation into light*. She pictures its structure as a circle which emits *eternal light*, below which *time can be glimpsed*. In addition to the pen pals describing the twilight in Blaenhonddan and Ljósvallagata, they also discuss light in many subsequent letters. *I'm trying to understand light*, my grandaunt writes in one of them, *how it is turned on, how it turns off*.

In one of Gwynvere's last letters, written some twenty years after my grandaunt declared she had started her research, it can be gleaned that for a period my grandaunt intended to change the title of *The Truth about Light* to *Mother of Light*. Her pen pal liked the title and it gave her the opportunity to explain that the first part of her name, Gwyn, derives from a Welsh word that means white or bright.

My sister has asked me if I can use the letters to date the manuscripts and put them in the right order, but it's not that simple both because drafts of my grandaunt's letters are undated and because she has a tendency to jump from

134

the subject matter of one manuscript to another in the same letter. In addition to which *the light which burrows into the world* crops up in all of the manuscripts, often in unexpected places. *The history of man is the history of millions of light refractions* is a phrase to be found in *Animal Life*, for example.

As in the other manuscripts, the emphasis of the subject matter shifts from being poetic, even prophetic in places, to being scientific. The introduction to *The Truth about Light* is fairly typical of her treatment of the material. At the beginning, my grandaunt speculates on what she calls the *dual nature* of light (later in the script she talks about the *twofold nature* of light), i.e. whether light is waves or photons or even both. She then quotes Jorge Luis Borges and asks *Is it an empire, this light that is going out, or a firefly's glow?* This is followed by statistical data on sunrises and sunsets in Reykjavík in June and December:

24 December 11:22 (sunrise) 15:32 (sunset)
21 June 02:54 (sunrise) 24:04 (sunset)

(She has added Akureyri 21 June in brackets: 01:25 (sunrise) 01:03 (sunset).)

She then says she has come to realize that light is considerably more complex than man and ends the introduction with: *This is my ode to light, this is a book about darkness.*

I'm also intrigued to discover that the manuscript contains an entire chapter on electricity and the history of the electrification of Iceland, which she traces back to Magnús Stephensen, who was the first to demonstrate the *properties of electricity* in 1793. She focuses a great deal on the Icelandic word for electricity, which Magnús initially referred to as electrical energy and Jónas Hallgrímsson subsequently changed to electric power and Konráð Gíslason finally ended up calling electricity or *rafmagn* in his dictionary. She also specifies that in the early years electricity was sold per bulb socket. *That meant that people paid a certain fee for each bulb connection they had in their houses*, my grandaunt writes.

Did you reach any conclusions on light? Gwynvere asks in one of her letters. *Did you accomplish your mission?*

From the draft of her reply letter, it can be inferred that my grandaunt believes that man both turns on light and turns off light. *He turns on and off. Off and on*, she writes and explains: *It can be likened to when a child fiddles with a switch and doesn't know why or what his intentions are.*

"Is Fifa any closer to figuring out the relationship between man and light?" my sister asks.

"She considers man to be a like a child playing with a light switch," I say.

That reminds me that when my grandaunt and I were driving through Grafarvogur, a voice in the passenger seat could be heard saying:

"Some people bring light with them, Dýja dear. Others try to drag you into their darkness. They're not necessarily able to control it."

On a vertical journey through the moment

Vaka and her female friends soon appear and carry the furniture out onto the landing, and then down the stairs and out to the trailer marked with a rescue squad logo. One member of the group is her co-tenant. In the end they also take one of the chests of drawers, which I first empty.

They tell me that the tourist in the loft was on his way in and helped them load the sofa onto the trailer.

I had already sorted through my duplicate possessions in the kitchen and arranged them on the dining table, including, among other things, two ladles, two cheese slicers, two rolling pins and two gravy boats. I also laid out one of the three sets of cups and saucers that came with the apartment and sat in the cupboard unused.

My colleague picks up a saucer and examines it.

"I wouldn't have the heart to take this," she says, putting it back down again.

"It's called the Blue Onion, Czech. My granny had a set like that as well."

On their final trip they nevertheless take a box full of kitchen utensils.

After everything has been loaded onto the trailer, the apartment seems to have grown bigger.

But it has also revealed patches of peeling paint and faded wallpaper in the places where the furniture had stood.

"It needs to be painted," is my colleague's verdict. She adds, "I can help you if you like. It's the least I can do for the furniture."

I mention the electrician's idea of removing the partition between the dining room and kitchen to open up the space between them.

"He said it wasn't there originally," I say.

She taps the wall and says that we'd only have to loosen a few screws and that she'll come back with a drill later.

The sleet has turned into rain and when it rains it sometimes leaks into the loft. Three years ago, scaffolding was raised at the back of the building when the roof had to be repaired and the plan was to repair the windows in the attic. The carpenters haven't been seen since, but the scaffolding is still standing there. The editor downstairs regularly phones the construction company and they're always on their way, but then something crops up. It has also occurred to me that the electricity problems might be somehow connected to leaks in the house. Between the chimneys on the block, there is a taut cable that was originally connected to old TV aerials, but hasn't been removed. On several occasions birds have crashed against the cable, because they've aimed badly, been blinded by the sun or reflections of silver hoar frost off the corrugated-iron roof. Vigorous fluttering is heard and tremors in the air as they tumble. Not long ago, in fact, a migrating bird smashed into the wire and plummeted onto the path by the dustbins on a vertical spin through the moment. I came home just as my neighbour was checking on it. We stood on the path, examining the bird as it lay in a small pool of blood and feathers. It had a peculiar orange crest, a kind of tassel, on the crown of his head and we couldn't identify the species. My neighbour thought it was a strange coincidence that the bird had hit the sidewalk as she was taking her rubbish out because she had just finished editing a book about migratory birds. She put the creature in a bag and said she was going to show it to an ornithologist, who had worked with her on the book. The next time I met her, she told me it was a bird that normally lived in more southerly regions and one that had never been spotted here before. Most likely, it had been blown across the ocean. She repeated what a bizarre coincidence it had been that this feathered creature should have crashed onto planet earth after such a long and perilous journey the day after the book on migratory birds had gone to the printers. Otherwise she could have included it.

It occurs to me that I could have told the tourist about the birds that occasionally get blown across the North Atlantic ocean when he asked me how windy windy was.

Behold, light breaks

The woman who serves me in the paint department asks how large a surface I need to paint and I tell her I'm going to paint a bedroom and the living room. She asks what colour and I ask for white. She asks if I want *frost white, marble white, salt white, snow white, all white, cotton white, lime white, pearl white* or *shell white*?

I go for *frost white*.

"White reflects all wavelengths of light," she says, scrutinizing me.

I then remember that there is wallpaper on one of the walls in the dining room. She says it's easy to peel that off and hands me a bottle of liquid I'm supposed to spray on the wallpaper so it comes off in strips. It occurs to me that I could also paint the kitchen. She wants to know what kind of fittings there are and if there are tiles. I tell her there are amber tiles in the kitchen. "From 1970," I add. And say they've started to look worn. She says she can picture them, the tiles, and recommends that I roll paint over them, after cleaning them with a degreasing agent. She advises me to paint the cupboard doors as well and spreads out a colour chart. In the next department I can buy new handles. As she talks, I sense there's something weighing on her. Occasionally she seems to be on the point of changing the subject, as if she were about to say something that has nothing to do with paint or tiles.

When she's finished stacking the cans of paint on the counter and fetching trays, rollers and brushes, she smiles at me.

I smile back at her.

"You delivered the four-kilo girl I had in March. It was a thirty-six-hour delivery."

She hesitates.

"I wanted to thank you for the poem you read to me in the delivery room. It was about leaves and their meshes of veins which the sun shone through."

She gets a bottle of oil to varnish the dining room table.

"Since then I've bought three books of poetry and also taken some out at the library."

I'm struck by how many poets wax lyrical about trees. They go walking through woods, stand under leafy crowns, twigs snap under their feet, they hear the rustle of dry leaves, they lose themselves in dark greenwoods, they visit autumn woodlands and deserted forests, leaves tremble in the wind, wither and fall.

I have to protect my hands and therefore buy two pairs of gloves.

On my way home, I also recall that when I had finished reading the poem, she had asked if it said what kind of tree it was.

"Does it say what kind of tree it is?" she asked.

"No, it's not specified by name."

"Could it be an oak?"

"Yes, it could be an oak."

In fact in *The Truth about Light* there is a chapter with a lengthy discussion on oak trees in relation to the human lifespan. Comparisons between man and various species of

141

plants and trees are given a great deal of weight in the manuscript and, as might be expected, my grandaunt emphasizes the fact that considering the lifespan of an oak tree, man is a mere mayfly. *Oak trees can be five hundred years old, which is seven times a human's lifespan. An oak tree that was planted back in the day of Elizabeth I still stands. This wise old oak in the forest has survived many wars and plagues that have wiped out entire counties. Famous poets have stood under this oak and written sonnets, conspiracies to treason and betrayals have been concocted there, lovers have held their rendezvous and children have been conceived, not all legitimately.* I cannot help being struck by the closing words of her speculations about the oak tree: *When that tree was planted man had not yet invented the word coincidence and Pascal had yet to be born.*

Insects

My sister phones when I'm almost home and says she has bought me a floor lamp as a Christmas gift.

"You can adjust the shade so that it lights up the corners and ceiling."

She next asks me where I am and what I'm doing.

I tell her I've been buying paint and that I'm on Hringbraut road on my way home.

"Opposite the old folks' home."

She asks whether I'm going to start painting three days before Christmas and I say I'm getting some help.

"Vaka and her friends from the rescue squad offered."

I wonder if she's going to mention the weather. She saves that for last and says that the forecast is still "changing and surprising".

"We don't know how bad the weather will be at this stage. It could be better than the worst-case scenario or worse than the best-case scenario."

She lowers her voice.

"It's clearly not just a question of securing loose objects; we can also expect power lines to go down."

I run into the tourist when I get home and he holds the hall door open for me and my buckets of paint. He's drenched to the bone with water trickling down his hair. He says he was out sightseeing and offers to carry a bucket of paint upstairs and asks if I'm working on something. I tell him I'm painting the apartment. On the way up he says he's pleased with the darkness and is excited to see how the stars arrange themselves in our sky. It strikes me as odd that he should say he's *pleased with the darkness*, and I think of the fact that there hasn't been a clear sky for two weeks and no stars have been visible. Then he says that he found a small spider in the bathroom hanging on a single thread and that was the only insect he'd spotted so far.

Not long ago I remember reading a news report about millions of spiders raining down on a town in Australia where houses, fields and people were shrouded in cobwebs. There were huge floods in the area and, to avoid drowning, the spiders had clung to the tallest vegetation. Their self-preservation effort involved weaving a complex mesh of webs that rose from the plants high into the sky and the spiders then used the wind to travel between places in the atmosphere.

"If you need anyone to hold onto the ladder, don't hesitate to ask," he says, handing me the paint.

All of a sudden I ponder how likely it is that he will offer to warm my cold hands?

I lean against the door frame and the bell that has been out of order for more than a year suddenly rings.

The conclusion

The rescue squad has dragged the furniture away from the walls, rolled up the carpet with the golden roses, taken down the tapestry of the Virgin Mary and baby Jesus and laid it on the double bed. They've also dismantled most of the partition between the kitchen and the living room and are busy carrying the panels out onto the path. I turn to the kitchen and unscrew the handles of the cupboard. The screwdriver is kept in the drawer with the bulbs and torch. I then follow the painting department's recommendation and sand the cupboard doors. This takes the gloss off and brightens the wood by a few shades. A horizontal shaft of sunshine pierces through the kitchen window, projecting a small square box of light on the wall beside the Eimskip calendar. In the two hours that follow, the light box travels across the wall.

I can't help thinking of Aunty Fífa.

"How many people don't stand by the window in the morning, Dýja dear, waiting for dawn to break or in the evening waiting for it to grow dark?"

Looking back, I feel my grandaunt was increasingly preoccupied with coincidences and saw them everywhere. As far as I can make out, she considered coincidence to be the most important concept in the history of evolution.

"Notice the coincidence, Dýja dear," she used to say.

Man owes his life to many coincidences, my grandaunt writes in a brief and fragmentary preface to her *Coincidence* manuscript. *The most important of all is our own conception, but I have also come to realize that coincidences play a major role in most of the things that matter in life.*

Coincidence also happens to be the manuscript I have the most difficulties coming to terms with. In the final chapter which she calls *Conclusions*, she falls very short of reaching a conclusion. On the contrary, chaos reigns more than ever. I've tried to explain to my sister that our grandaunt seemed to believe that coincidences are mostly to be found in the details. What's more, these details determine the directions our lives take. To her mind, details was just another word for fundamentals. *The smallest unit of time is not a moment, but rather a moment is inhabited by many moments and within every moment lies a coincidence, which determines our entire life.*

This reminds me of when we were in the car driving back south, after my grandaunt and I had finished, as my sister described it, rummaging through the piles of bones of distant relatives, she harped on about how this or that deceased ancestor had come into being as the result of an accident or miracle. It was a coincidence that this one had met that one and a certain foremother or forefather was created, no offspring was supposed to come of it, it hadn't been part of the plan, certain individuals weren't supposed to meet, least of all become lovers, many forefathers and many foremothers were also almost dead by the time they managed to reproduce, a pregnant foremother considered throwing herself into a river glistening in the twilight; this demonstrated how little it would often have taken for us not to have existed, what an extraordinary coincidence it was that we were sitting side by side in the Lada, in the middle of Hrútafjord, she and her fifty-five-years younger travelling companion; yes, the fact that we should have encountered each other was a coincidence upon a coincidence, many generations of coincidences.

"Hundreds of millions of sperms competed to fertilize one egg," the former midwife concluded in her appraisal of the coincidence of existence.

When I've given the kitchen fittings a coat of varnish, they're as good as new. I then turn to scraping the paper off the dining room walls. There seem to be three coats of different-coloured paint underneath. The squad has finished filling the holes in the bedroom wall and has almost finished painting the first coat in the living room.

The sun now hangs low in the sky, at eye level through the window, and in a golden cluster between two spruce trees in the graveyard, just above the tombs, sunrays briefly glisten.

The days are still growing shorter. Then they will start lengthening again tomorrow.

Coincidences weren't invented until 1605

Coincidences feature prominently in the correspondence between the two pen pals, Gwynvere and my grandaunt, and they discuss back and forth *the bizarre causality between events that occur without any visible connection. Is coincidence perhaps God?* Gwynvere asks, but I can't determine from the drafts whether my grandaunt answers the question or not.

In one of the letters, my grandaunt talks about the male midwife she had found and was going to write about: Gísli Raymond, who was never called anything other than Nonni. Here I lost the thread because, by this stage, my grandaunt seemed to have stopped writing rough drafts of her letters. A letter from her pen pal in Wales, however, contains information about a certain Raymond Nonnatus, who was the patron saint of midwives, pregnant women and childbirth, and the note begins with the following words: *To continue on the theme of coincidence, which is so dear to you…* She explains

147

that the mother of the saint died giving birth to him and he was delivered by Caesarean section. *Nonnatus means he who is not born*, Gwynvere writes in big wavy letters on light blue transparent airmail paper.

Coincidence also crops up in the last letter my grandaunt writes to Gwynvere, which was returned to her. In it, among other things, she says:

When I was searching for the word coincidence in the dictionary of Shakespeare's beautiful native language, dear Gwynvere, I discovered that the term wasn't invented until 1605.

When man is gone,
the light will remain

My sister still occasionally asks:

"Are you still going through Fífa's papers?"

"Yes, I've been typing them into the computer."

"Isn't it a waste of time?"

"Yes, probably."

For a long time I considered that *Animal Life, Investigation into what the human species is capable of*, was most likely the oldest manuscript, but I hesitated on whether *Coincidence* or *The Truth about Light* was the youngest. The last time my sister asked me what stage I'd reached in sorting out the papers and whether I was getting any closer, I said that I thought our grandaunt was initially trying to understand human behaviour, but had then given up and changed course and decided to try to understand light instead. And that she had then stopped writing about light and started to write about coincidence.

"Or the other way around," I said. "Gave up on coincidence and decided to write about light instead. I'm not sure of the chronology."

After a while it dawned on me that she might have been working on all three manuscripts at once.

One of the indicators I've tried to use in dating the manuscripts is my grandaunt's waning faith in humankind. In *Animal Life* other animals fare well without humans and soon, from the middle of *The Truth about Light* onwards, plants fare well without humans, although humans cannot survive without the plants. Finally, the world fares admirably without humans in *Coincidence*, which I've long considered to be the final manuscript. To complicate things, however, in all of the manuscripts my grandaunt actually ponders whether man has a place in the world or whether he is perhaps redundant.

Man thinks the birds sing for him, but when he vanishes, forests will grow again and animals will thrive, and birds will continue to fly between continents, across borders and oceans, and nest in peat bogs between two tussocks or in swamps or the edge of cliffs. They will no longer have to share the berries with man because he will have ceased to make jams and juices. This is followed by a long exposition of birds' flying skills in a kind of fusion of biology and physics. She mentions the different shapes of wings and their sizes in

149

relation to their bodies. Those with larger wingspans, such as the Arctic tern, can fly the longest distances. Other birds, though, have greater difficulties flying and need to take a run to get themselves off the ground and are heavy in the air, like geese. Others, like the puffin, use the rising air currents off the edge of cliffs to soar. The most remarkable feature of these creatures, however, is undoubtedly their bird's-eye view. Finally, she wonders what meaning the words world and home might have once man has vanished from the planet. She asks: *is the home of migratory birds the place where they spend the winter or where they lay eggs and raise their young?*

My aunt's conclusion is clear: Everything indicates that *man will be the most short-lived species on earth.*

When man is gone, the light will remain, my grandaunt writes in *The Truth about Light.*

If, on the other hand, I were to focus on style to determine the chronology, I could well believe that *The Truth about Light* was the last manuscript. In *Coincidence* it is more than likely that my grandaunt chose her topics haphazardly, as if she were pulling tickets out of a hat, whereas in the section about light, the text seems to falls apart and dissolve in the end. Blank spaces on the pages multiply and there are longer gaps between the sentences and words; ultimately the connection between letters in individual words is broken, leaving them to stand on their own. I browse through page after page of virtually blank sheets and wonder whether they actually form part of the manuscript or are there by accident. On the last pages there are a few words scattered here and there until I come to the last ones:

Under
a new
sky
new
earth
a   b   i   r   d
is   h e a r d.

I originally thought the manuscript, which the publisher had rejected, had to be *Animal Life*, the volume about what humans are capable of, but I'm now leaning more towards thinking that it was the most disjointed manuscript, *The Truth about Light*, in which man has disappeared and the light stays behind without him.

Patterns of human behaviour

It wasn't until recently that I came across some curled-up tracing paper among the boxes of buttons and pin cushions in the bottom drawer of the chest, an entire roll in fact, which has puzzled me somewhat. When I unrolled it, I discovered many pencil drawings that had been stuck together with tape. I assumed they were drafts of embroidery patterns, but there didn't seem to be any discernible model or obvious structure or design, no system; rather it was as if the drawings had been improvised and my grandaunt had added sheets on a whim. In certain places she had jotted down on the paper the embroidery method and colour of the yarn: cross stitch, violet backstitch, green flat seam, hooked stitch, contour stitch, duplicate stitch, running stitch. It all seemed to indicate that the intention had been to mix different kinds of stitches and embroidery methods, because she included both long stitches and short ones, stitches that were braided and stitches that were interlaced. In some places sharp turns were taken and then changed direction halfway. What struck me the most were the large blank spaces in which my grandaunt had scribbled the word *light*. The gaps seemed to multiply as more sheets were added and, at the same time, it was as if the forms started to unravel and the work became increasingly unfathomable. When I unfolded the entire drawing and spread it out on the desk, the image conjured up in my mind was that of footprints left by a flock of blackbirds over a thin covering of snow on my grandaunt's grave. At the top of the page a trembling hand had written:

Patterns of human behaviour.

I have not fully examined everything that my grandaunt left behind. I've only loosely been through what is stored in the basement, for example, but I haven't found any piece of embroidery that tallies with these drawings. I now vaguely recall her mentioning her "final piece" when I visited her in hospital and her saying that I should complete it. She spoke in riddles about final stitches, tying up loose ends and cutting the thread, and said I had the right hands for it. I thought she'd meant the midwifery work, a lot of what she said seemed to indicate that—stitches, sewing and the cord that connects a mother and child, as if I was some kind of extension to her work.

It has now occurred to me that the drawings are a continuation of the manuscript about light, that my grandaunt Fífa had ground to a halt and given up writing the manuscripts, that she had *run out of words*, as she put it, and intended to turn back to embroidering again. *I've given up on language*, my grandaunt writes in her last letter to her pen pal, the one that was returned after Gwynvere's death. And then she adds: *I've now completed an outline of a large embroidery work that I am going to do using a free method. The most difficult part will be to embroider the light.*

"No more words are needed," she said to me, "no more words in this world, Dýja dear."

Ulysses Breki

I'm finishing scraping the paper off the wall when the phone rings.

I think I hear the ocean, even surf and screeching birds.

"Ketill here."

"Ketill…?"

"The electrician."

He starts off by asking if any more bulbs have blown since yesterday.

"No, none," I say.

The connection breaks up every now and then, but I hear him say he needed fresh air and therefore went out for a drive. He had started off by just driving down the street and then across the neighbourhood, without quite knowing where he was going, and then he had driven aimlessly on and suddenly found himself in front of his mother's house, his childhood home, which had been sold, and after that he had taken the road east of the mountain, Þrengslin, until he had reached the village of Eyrarbakki. When he was opposite the Litla Hraun prison, he phoned Sædís to tell her he would be delayed. After that he had walked down to the shore and watched the surf. In actual fact he hadn't exactly watched the surf because there wasn't much to see in the darkness and snowfall so it was more a case of listening to the ocean, one could say.

He's now back in his car and heading towards town.

I ask about the baby. Then the mother.

He says the child is doing fine.

There is a prolonged silence on the line and I wonder if the connection has dropped.

"I know what Sædís will say when I return," he continues. "Every time I go out, she thinks I won't come back. That's what she'll say, I know you didn't want to come back."

"It's a lot of strain to take care of a baby," I say.

I hear him taking a deep breath.

"The thing is I wanted to know if you might be willing to pop over and talk to Sædís."

"What about the midwifery home service, like we talked about?"

"She agreed to you coming for a visit. You don't necessarily have to come as a midwife," he adds, "just as a person."

I think it over.

"She's constantly repeating that now that Ulysses Breki is born, he will also die. I tell her that he won't die straight away. That first he'll live. That he could live to the age of eighty-nine like her granddad. She says that whether it's straight away or not straight away isn't the issue. The point is he'll die. Then she asks if I want to make a person and then leave him behind in a world of droughts, pollution and viruses? I say to her, he's already born, Sædís."

I hear the car engine being turned off, followed by the opening and closing of a door.

"I'm at my wits' end," he ends up saying.

I tell him I'll be there in an hour.

I take down the curtain rail in the bedroom and remove the rings. The curtains have a pattern that looks like big raindrops falling vertically to the ground.

The rescue squad has grown in number, there are now four of them and they've started painting the bedroom.

To eat, drink, sleep, communicate, share, discover

They're in the same neighbourhood, at a walking distance, as he had repeated on the phone.

I worked in the home service for one summer and know what is awaiting me: a pale woman with white, bloodless lips, a corridor crammed with shoes, a stuffy apartment, closed windows, radiators up high, a new mother with sore breasts, a newborn with tummy aches, on the kitchen table an open pizza box, with one slice left. I say it straight out: pepperoni has a bad effect on the baby.

The electrician receives me on the steps, he leans the door back behind him and lowers his voice as he quickly brings me up to speed.

"My wife just cries and cries."

He hesitates.

"And I do too actually. We cry together. Is that normal?"

He doesn't say: "I'm like everyone else, I love, cry and suffer."

I say:

"It might be good to talk to a psychologist."

When I've finished washing my hands and greeting the woman, I bend over the cradle.

The baby is fast asleep. I think of a chapter in my grand-aunt's book about human development:

While a female seal will shake off its pup after six weeks, for the first weeks of its life, a human child does little more than sleep, drink and expel waste.

I sit on a chair and ask how it's going.

I know what's going through her mind: she fears having to take care of a fragile unknown being and also fears that she will never be alone again.

"I was going to use the last summer in my life in which I'd be alone to go out camping and mountain trekking but I couldn't because I felt nauseated all the time," is the first thing she says.

I ponder. In my experience there are just as many women who are ready to have a child as those who are not.

The husband alternately looks at me and her. Then he decides to give us some privacy and vanishes into the kitchen. I hear him pottering about, running water and clanging dishes. He's washing up.

"I was going to stay up all night and watch the sun set and immediately rise again, but I couldn't stay awake any later than nine thirty at night. I was going to pitch a tent by a stream and cook on a Primus. I was going to climb Mt Esja."

The baby sneezes. They wake up when they sneeze.

Another chapter in *Animal Life* comes to mind: *Human offspring develop slower than other animals.*

157

It takes a human child two to three months to manage to hold their heads steady and to smile back at the faces that smile at them and about as long for them to discover that they have hands.

"You can also do some of that next summer," I say. "You can watch the sun set and immediately rise again and go on a mountain walk." I add, "You can take some cocoa in a flask and lean against a rock and look over the strait."

She sighs.

"By the time I stopped feeling nauseated, I was too heavy to go mountain hiking. Autumn had arrived and it had snowed on Mt Esja."

The baby yawns and winces.

I hear the electrician opening the hall door, crunches in the snow, the slamming lid of a dustbin and, after a brief moment, he is back inside again and closes the door behind him. He has taken the rubbish out. I give him a sign and he walks over to the woman and pats her on the shoulder. He has an apron wrapped around him.

When he follows me out onto the steps, he leans the door back as he had done when he received me. It's bitingly cold.

"Now do you understand what I mean?" he says.

He looks beyond me towards the sky and clasps his hands, as if to rub life into them. Then he sticks them into the pockets of his trousers.

"Earlier on, when I took the rubbish out, my neighbour's cat appeared and brushed against my feet and purred," he says, but the topic soon turns back to his wife. "I try to take care of her so she can take care of the baby. I tell her 'isn't it enough to be alive, Sædís? To eat, drink, sleep, communicate, share, discover?' 'Preferably before the sun burns out,' she answered."

He dabs his eyes with the sleeve of the chequered shirt protruding from his sweater.

I give him an emergency number to call.

Revolution, bread, time, doubt, justice, truth, an island, suffering, courage

When the squad have gone home and I'm alone, I open the wardrobe and lay my grandaunt's dresses out on the bed, one after another, and fold them up. I divide them into three piles: Mothers' Support Committee, Red Cross and Salvation Army. I keep two dresses, one is green with a belt, the other black with a pearly lace collar. I try on the black one. It needs to be taken in around the waist and the chest, so I fetch the pin cushion and stick in a few stitch markers before slithering out of it again.

On a number of occasions I've found myself delivering the babies of former lovers of mine. I was on duty when the man who was supposed to become the father of my child showed up at the maternity ward two years after we'd parted ways. The birth was in full progress and

I directed him to his wife in the examination room and greeted them both with a handshake. He held my hand for a prolonged moment and I sensed insecurity, then I had to rush out but he immediately followed behind, running up to me.

I said I was going to get another midwife.

"There's no need," he said. And he hesitantly added: "How are you doing?"

"Fine."

I also asked him how he was doing.

"Good," he said.

I last met him unexpectedly in the swimming pool a few days ago. He was holding the hand of a little girl with inflatable wings on her arms, leading her around the pool and escorting her to a shallow tub where kids were pottering about and he stood there for a moment, watching over her. I was sitting in the hot tub and saw him heading towards it. He made his way down the steps into the hot water, closing his eyes and keeping them shut for a while. Then he opened them again to keep an eye on the child. The girl waved at him and he waved back. It was only then he spotted me and struggled to find the words:

"Are you still working at the maternity ward?"

I told him I was. In addition to the fourteen-year-old boy I had delivered and the girl who was splashing around with the other kids and had momentarily forgotten her father, he said he also had a one-year-old daughter.

He allowed himself to sink deeper into the water, up to his chin.

When he straightened up again, he looked at me and asked:

"And you, do you have any kids?"

"No, no kids," I said.

Then he had to check on his daughter. She was fine.

I met the pair of them again at the entrance when I was returning the key, and he pulled out photographs of his other two kids to show me.

At two o'clock in the morning, I finish painting the first coat in the dining room. I then put the lid back on the can of paint and rinse the rolls. I think I hear some movement in the loft and it occurs to me that the tourist from the other side of the planet might be awake.

When I'd bumped into him on the stairs the other day, he'd said he had trouble sleeping, because of jet lag. He also said he'd realized that it's impossible to read during the day without turning a light on. Then he asked if people read out in the gardens in the summer and I thought to myself this isn't a country where gentle breezes rustle pages and clouds drift by and dance on poetry.

"It's not very common for people to read outside," I said.

Now I feel uncertain as to whether or not I placed enough emphasis on how wild the weather is going to get.

I fall asleep, but a short while later wake with a jolt to the sound of a fly buzzing in the room and turn on the bedside lamp. I then get up to fetch some poetry books from the shelf and browse through them in search of a horizon. There are so many things that poets have conjured up on the furthest skyline: boats, the sun, distant lands, revolution, bread, time, doubt, justice, truth, an island, suffering, courage.

Black hole

I lie in bed and the window frame casts a shadow on the wall by the bed, drawing a cross.

Before the rescue squad left yesterday, they helped to move the desk out of the bedroom into the spot in the living room where the sofa had stood. It fits perfectly beside the bookcase. Once the desk was out, I could move the bed so that it would be easier to open the bedroom door. Today I rearranged the books.

"I couldn't help noticing that you had an artificial Christmas tree and a box of decorations in the other room," said Vaka when we were alone again.

She suggested we put up the tree. I went to fetch it and she held the box with the Christmas decorations.

She was spellbound.

"This is like something out of the National Museum."

I run downstairs to grab the newspaper and swiftly skim through it, as I make toast. A brief article attracts my attention, but it's the photograph that accompanies it that strikes me the most.

The headline reads: *In the middle of a black hole there is light.*

The article explains that they've managed to photograph a black hole for the first time and it revealed that at the centre of a black hole there is light. The photograph isn't very clear but it shows a nebulous spotted area—for some reason the ultrasound scan image of a womb springs to mind— and in the middle of it there is a brighter circular opening, like the end of a long corridor.

My grandaunt had been on the right track. Those were precisely the words she used in one of her letters to Gwynvere, that she was *on the right track. In the middle of darkness, the heart of darkness, there is light*, she writes.

I hear shuffling on the landing and a moment later there is a knock on the door. I tie my hair in an elastic band and go to the door. My neighbour from the loft stands outside with folded bedclothes which he hands me and thanks me for lending.

"I've ironed them," he says.

He shows no sign of leaving so I invite him in. He strokes the vinyl wallpaper in the hallway and says his granny had similar wallpaper in her place.

Glancing around the living room, he pauses by the bookcase and pulls out a volume of poems by Borges and says, "I've got this book too."

He then flicks through my record collection and halts on Liszt's "Consolation No. 3 in D flat major" and says, "I've got this record as well." Next, he moves to the window and gazes outside. A seagull with a yellow beak and ragged feathers perches on a lamp post. I watch it glide down to the sidewalk and prowl between the cars in the flaxen light. I'd left the living room window open last night to get rid of the smell of paint and a white patina of snow has formed. It occurs to me that I need to repot the begonia.

"I felt a slight glimmer of sunshine coming through the window earlier," he says, "a red streak, just for a brief moment."

I adjust my grandaunt's bracelet. Turn it on my wrist. The Christmas tree stands on the carpet with the yellow golden roses. I've never put up Christmas decorations before.

I ask him when his son's birthday is and he answers July the seventeenth.

"He was born in the heart of winter," he adds.

I ask if he's sensitive.

"Yeah, just like his mother," he answers.

I ask him if he makes breakfast for his son and he says he does.

I ask him if he fears for him and he says he does.

Then I suddenly remember the fragment of a dream I had last night where, just as I was awaking, I felt I could hear my aunt's voice say: *all men are damaged by life, Dýja dear.*

164

The tourist is standing right by my shoulder and I think what now, what's next?

He didn't see the light

I have one more shift before Christmas Eve; I clock in and put on my uniform. Two midwives, who have just finished their night shift, sit dejectedly in the staffroom. I notice one of them has been crying. The watch supervisor greets me with a grave air and beckons me into the office. It transpires that a fully mature baby died at birth during the night and I'm to take over with the woman who lost the child.

"She specifically asked for you," she says.

She looks at me.

"She says she met you in the hall when she was checking in for the birth and that you helped her in the elevator."

I think for a moment.

"But that was three days ago," I say. "Was she only giving birth last night?" I ask.

"Yes, seems so. It was a protracted labour."

I hear her say that messages got muddled between shifts and she uses the word misunderstanding. That there was a misunderstanding.

She continues.

"There has yet to be a meeting to go over the work procedures."

There is a brief silence, then she adds:

"They don't want a priest."

"When will she be discharged?"

"There were no plans to discharge her before tomorrow but she wants to go home."

She hesitates.

"She isn't crying."

I knock gently on the door to the room and open it.

The woman is sitting up in her bed, staring into her hands. She has taken a shower and her hair is wet. A tray with an untouched breakfast lies on the table. Porridge, a slice of buttered bread with cheese.

A refrigerated cuddle cot stands by the bed with the child inside.

The father is sitting on a chair beside it, looking at the baby. When I enter, he stands up and walks over to the window. In doing so he brushes against me and apologizes.

"Sorry," he says.

He stands by the window for a brief moment and gazes out at the parking lot. He then gathers the woman's clothes and lays them on the bed. He leaves to fetch two grannies and one granddad to give them a chance to say goodbye to the child.

I move the chair and sit beside the woman.

"We haven't told his sister yet that her brother won't be coming home with us," is the first thing she says.

"Your darling little boy," I say.

"She's learning the neuter gender at school," she continues.

I remove the needles from the back of her hand.

"He struggled to survive for a long time," she says, without looking at the cot.

I sit by her and remain silent.

The baby seat for the car sits on the floor.

"Last night there were two hearts beating inside me."

When she speaks, she plucks at her hair, as if she were untangling it with her fingers, like a harpist.

"They weighed him and he was three kilos and seven hundred and fifty grams, and fifty-two centimetres long. He was ready. A big boy with big hands. I'll never get to find out if he was dyslexic like his dad."

She speaks.

I remain silent.

"They washed his hair and dried it. It was curly," she says, and lets her feet sink to the floor and starts to get dressed. Her shoes stand on the floor by the bed, black walking ankle boots with a zipper on the side.

"I heard someone say that he was lying on the left side."

She puts on her shoes.

"Now I understand why I couldn't lie on my left side."

When I get home I run a bath. Then I allow myself to sink into the water, to sink into the darkest depths, into the place we come from, out of the murky pool of the beginning.

I'm trying to understand fleeting and dangerous phenomena such as life itself, my grandaunt writes in a letter to her pen pal Gwynvere.

Every life that is ignited is a universe. Every life that is extinguished is a universe.

Doesn't live here any more

"Have you reached any conclusions on Fífa's studies?" my sister asks.

"Yes and no."

"Does she have any faith in humans?"

"She both does and she doesn't."

"Is there hope?"

"There's hope and there isn't hope."

I start thinking about a chapter in *Animal Life* called *Man's last days on earth.*

"I think she believes that man will inevitably wipe himself out," I add.

My grandaunt's writing isn't without paradox, though. It repeatedly happens that her opinions in one chapter are contradicted by her opinions in another. I could tell my sister that our grandaunt mistrusts her own narrative, that she constantly doubts her own knowledge and undermines it. Or she thinks of an alternative approach that could shed new light on the issue. It occurs to me that she didn't want to come to a conclusion, because nothing is black and white enough to be unequivocally resolved, because no words are absolute. I suspect she might have been referring to her own mindset when she wrote to Gwynvere: *It's possible to have an opinion on everything. And the opposite opinion.*

In my grandaunt's final letter to Gwynvere, which was returned to her marked *doesn't live here any more*, the following words are to be found:

You ask me if I'm any closer. The answer to that is no. It's more a case of knowing less today than yesterday. I know, of course, that the sun rises and sets, that man is born and dies, that nothing is final or immutable and that man is an explorer in a world of eternally shimmering and changeable light.

Further down she writes:

It's difficult to understand another person. But what is even more difficult to understand, difficult to know, what is most alien of all that is alien, unknown of all that is unknown, is one's self.

"So there's no conclusion?"

Throughout my long life I've tried to find out why a man is born. I finally understand it, I understand it now, I feel I see it all clearly: man is born to love.

"The most important quality in a human being, Dýja dear, is courage," my grandaunt once said to me. It tallies with a note she wrote with a pen in a margin of *Animal Life*: *the final words in the book should be about fortitude and courage.*

169

As he is dying, a poet asks his best friend,
a small stream,
"Will you remember me, eh?"

It was by coincidence that I was alone with my grandaunt when she died, ninety-three years old, half a month after suffering a heart attack. I visited her every day and sat with her and felt she was getting better. In fact she complained about no longer being able to recognize her own heartbeat after she had been given some new pills.

"That's not my beat any more," she said.

She'd asked me to bring in her perfume, which she kept in the bathroom cabinet. I unscrewed the top of *Scent of the Stars* and she sniffed the bottle and dabbed a few drops behind her ears. She then screwed the top back on and asked me to put the bottle back.

Mom had just left and my grandaunt sat up in bed, discussing life and existence, and I remember she asked me, as usual, how my shift had gone, how many babies had been born. She wanted to hear more about the innovations, what my opinion was on birthing pools, or the swimming pools which women gave birth in, as she put it. She then wanted to know if I had remembered to water the begonia. Half a cup a day is enough, she said. She also asked me to mind the box for her until she came home and I didn't give much thought to what box she meant.

I held her hand.

"It's important to rejoice," she said and smiled, "in our good fortune at having been born."

It was coming up to coffee time and she wanted me to go out to fetch her a cup and a slice of marital bliss cake. She said she was going to lie back for a short while and I helped adjust her pillow.

"I'm so grateful," I hear her say.

Thinking back on it, I found it odd when she added: "It was fun to experience this life."

When I came back she was dead.

Before I'd left to get the coffee she'd patted the back of my hand with two fingers as was her custom, with her index and middle finger, and said: "Coincidences, Dýja dear. Don't forget to keep an eye on the coincidences." Then she said, and I remember it very clearly: "I'll look after your boy."

Everything that is smaller than small

Even though my grandaunt didn't believe in man, she believed in the child. Or, to be more precise, she didn't believe in man, except in the period when he was fifty centimetres long. This also tallies with accounts given by her colleagues in the maternity division. On one hand, there was the person and, on the other, there was the child. Everything that was small and preferably even smaller than small, vulnerable and weak, stirred her interest and warmth, regardless of whether it belonged to the human, animal or plant kingdom, the young ones of every species, all newborns, whether they were kittens, lambs, day-old foals, the first dandelion of spring, the fragile eggs of birds, chicks in a nest, houseflies or bees, even a burgeoning potato awoke a sense of wonder and beauty in her; small berries seemed better to her than large ones bursting with sweetness, seeds and buds were preferred to fully sprouted plants; she rejoiced over the thin light-green shoots that grew out of stalks and felt them with her fingers, thinness is a great indicator, she said. Her mind was also preoccupied by any part of nature that was imperilled, by the animals and plants who were deceived by the promise of an imminent spring, with a transparent cold light, which forced its way into all nooks and crannies, but then vanished without warning under a white mound of snow, just as the trees were beginning to bud and the lambing season was at its peak. The paradox of the manuscripts was that, even though humans were expected to vanish from the earth, my grandaunt foresaw that the future kingdom would include, in addition to animals and plants, space for children. And not only them, because places were also supposed to be allotted to two other groups, as I tried to explain to my sister. On one hand, those who preserved the child within them and still *blew on dandelions and knew how to marvel* and, on the other hand—and this comes as no surprise, as my sister pointed out—poets.

Disjunction

Not long ago my sister asked me what I intended to do with the manuscripts.

Whether I was going to try to get them published.

Initially, I felt they lacked a thread or coherence, but as my reading progressed, I found myself in a quandary, and felt that what I had previously experienced as chaos and disjointedness was precisely what constituted the idea behind the work, its goal and purpose. That its organization was to be found in its disorganization, that there was a system to the chaos.

I try to explain to my sister that the structure of the work, with its peculiar collage of fragmented elements, is consistent with our grandaunt's ideas about the nature of humanity and their unpredictable behaviour, in accordance with a life, which was, above all else, at the mercy of the whims of that phenomenon she called coincidence. In light of this, it is precisely logical that there should be a lack of logical continuity in the writing. The coherence resides in the incoherence.

"I therefore assume there are no grounds for publication?" my sister asks.

"No, I don't think so."

In fact it comes as little surprise that my grandaunt couldn't find a publisher for such a peculiar and disjointed collection of material. One could say that I fully understood why the work had been rejected.

173

I also invested a considerable amount of time into working out which of the manuscripts was the last one and whether it was final until I realized that there was no final manuscript. Or rather that all of the manuscripts were the final manuscript. To be more precise, that the truth resided in the collective contents of the Chiquita box and that everything that was to be found there would therefore have to be published.

"It's actually a work in progress," I said. "Fífa never finished it."

"So you've stopped going through the papers?"

"Yes."

After ringing off from my sister, I pack the manuscripts back into the box and seal it with masking tape. I then carry it down three floors and open the door to the storage room. When I shift some things on the shelf to make space for the box, seven cans of Ora fish balls appear.

The sun is setting on the horizon and the sky is a blaze of bloody flames. After a brief moment, the world has turned into a puddle of black ink.

The Christmas parcels for my sister and family sit wrapped on the dining table.

My case

When I awake in the morning the smell of paint has diminished.

I'm preparing to go in for work when I get a call from the hospital. There have been quite a few changes in the personnel administration recently, with corresponding new job titles, and I hear the woman introduce herself as the newly appointed director of human resources.

I turn off the water.

She says she has been examining my case along with two other people she mentions by name, but whom I'm not familiar with, and that it has transpired that I've been taking a great deal of extra shifts lately. In addition to this, I haven't taken any full summer vacations over the past years.

"We also see you've taken a lot of the Christmas shifts over the past years."

There is a brief silence on the line before she continues.

"We agreed that it wasn't fair. That you work every Christmas. In fact you could take a vacation until mid-January."

"On salary?"

"Yes, you've accrued paid holidays."

I stand by the window and, as I'm talking to her, two birds fly against a black bank of clouds.

"Then there is one other thing," I hear the woman say. She hesitates.

175

"Regarding the couple who lost a baby..."

"Yes?"

"Whom you tended to yesterday."

"Yes."

She wants to know if I allowed the woman who lost the baby to take her file. Among other things, the printout from the monitor.

"Yes, I gave Margrét all the data about the birth. She asked for it."

"You should have asked for permission."

Apart from the luminous crosses in the graveyard, the world is still black.

The only certainty is uncertainty

As the day progresses, I notice a peculiar yellow glow in the air and, just as I do, my sister phones. She is on her way home from the Met Office and her voice is weary. She says that the depression is coming and it looks as if the storm will hit sooner than expected, around dinner time. The direction of the wind has also changed, which was something they hadn't expected.

"It now looks like it will be northerly winds and not westerly."

I tell her that it turns out that I've accumulated holidays and that I'll be on vacation over Christmas. She says that's good, but doesn't mention the dinner any further, and instead lowers her voice:

"We actually don't know what to expect."

I hear a tremor in her voice.

"The only certainty is uncertainty."

Nevertheless, she's put up the Christmas tree.

"As usual I decorated it on my own," she ends up saying.

Sky quake

The wind starts to pick up and thin veils of grey clouds tumble swiftly across the sky like fumes from a fire. People have drawn their curtains and stay warm in their apartments or windowless basements, if they're lucky enough to have one, as my sister says. There isn't a soul in sight in the neighbourhood. The sky has turned to the colour of lead and the wind is steadily mounting. The glass in the living room window buckles inwards and I back off a few steps, and stand by Mary and the child, while the shellfire pounds the windows. At an arm's length from me, a roof tile takes flight, followed by others, like a pack of cards scattering into the air. The noise precedes the onslaught, like the roar of an airplane preparing to land. I'm not sure which direction the storm is coming from any more; it seems to still be turning. The air pressure intensifies like labour contractions, and I see the tops of spruce trees swaying like the pendulums of clocks in the graveyard, how the trunks bend horizontally in the wind; the turbulence seems to last an eternity and the roots are nudged back and forth like teeth in a baby's gums until the deeply embedded sod starts to bulge and I see the giant roots being torn from their earthly connection and the tree trunks tumble headlong to the ground, one after another, like a film in slow motion. There will be no more growth rings on the oldest spruce tree in town, the habitat of three hundred pairs of blackbirds. The earth is a body in a straitjacket, then the wind eases its iron grip for a brief moment; for several seconds it's dead still, the stillness of death, in the eye of the hurricane, before the wind spirals up again and a new onslaught strikes the house. Around midnight the power cuts off in the neighbourhood and I fetch candles from the kitchen drawer.

I hear a shattering from the floor below, like a window being smashed to smithereens.

Is this the first or last day of the world?

I doze off late into the night and wake up in the morning. The storm is receding, but sunrise is still a long way off. I doze off again and dream that I'm standing alone in an arid wasteland, a brown barren sand desert, above me a high sky, in the distance a black lava field. Is the sun visible or is the sun not visible? I feel I'm standing under a rainbow, which suddenly changes into a multi-coloured disco ball spinning over a dance floor and I dance alone to *Born to Die*.

When I wake up again, it's almost noon and I lie in bed and can't recall the whole dream, but I do remember: the beat of a helicopter's rotor blades, glistening Christmas tree lights and glaring brightness. And I feel as if I can hear Fífa saying *bees dance intricate dances*.

I listen out for sounds and think I hear the howling of a dog. Then the banging of a hammer. I get up, walk to the window and open the curtains. It's perfectly calm and there is a flurry of snow.

When I step into the living room, for a moment I don't remember the visit last night when the tiles started to fly off the roof, and the guest, who is lying on the tasselled velvet sofa, asleep.

When it brightens properly, one can see that the window panes are white with salt stains and I'm struck by the devastation.

Scores of trees have snapped in the graveyard and the crosses are scattered all over like saplings. The earth's body is a gaping wound; its surface is torn and lacerated. Members of the rescue squad in orange overalls can be seen nailing boards over broken windows and securing roof tiles in various parts of the neighbourhood. The sky has crashed to earth and lies on the ground in a fluffy, soft white blanket.

179

The guest is awake and sits up. He folds the blanket and smiles at me. Then he walks over to the window. A helicopter hovers low over the graveyard.

I put some eggs in the pot.

"With us the bushes are burning and with you the roofs are flying off," he says.

Then he has to go upstairs to make a call.

"I promised," he says.

One of the trunks of the maple tree in the garden broke last night and crashed into the bedroom window of my neighbour on the second floor. I knock on her door and she shows me the damage. It was by chance that she happened to be in the kitchen, she says, and not in the bedroom at around midnight when the maple in the back garden collapsed, smashing the bedroom window. Or to be more precise one of the two trunks of the tree had broken loose like a gangway and fallen on the window. The other bole was left standing. The same can be said of the scaffolding which doesn't seem to have budged.

We both examine the shards of scattered glass and the torn curtains hanging in shreds.

"The strange thing," she says, "is that the plant on the windowsill didn't move."

When I'm back upstairs, I turn on the television and, as was to be expected, the news is full of reports about the damage the storm has caused. I watch an interview with the head of the civil defence department and footage of the rescue squad at work. For a moment, I think I see Vaka flash on the screen. It transpires that it wasn't just loose objects that took flight, not just roof tiles, but that entire rooftops flew away, a bus got blown into the pond, a crane was knocked over at the harbour and a minibus took off. I watch footage of ships capsizing in the harbour in the foamy waves and heavy surf crashing against the sky, and I listen to the woman reporter describe how the surge washed hundreds of kilos of boulders ashore and closed off streets in the city centre. A trawler has broken loose from the pier and been tossed against the harbour wall where it wavers with no lights on like a prehistoric iron animal. Many smaller boats have either sunk or drift like wrecks in the port. Finally, they say that the storm blew a hole in the harbour wall and that the carcass of a large whale, probably a sperm whale, was found half submerged in the sea close to the Harpa Concert Hall.

The world is just born

I hear the hall door open downstairs and, a moment later, my colleague in rescue squad overalls appears on the landing. It transpires she was called out all night. It occurs to me that she might want to lie down at my place, but she says she's on her way home and doesn't want to come in. She stands in the doorway and leans her head against the post, and says she has a little *favour* to ask of me, as she puts it. The problem is, she explains, shifting position, that she'd promised to take a northern lights excursion tonight. She closes her eyes briefly and then opens them again.

"A long time ago actually."

"Isn't the excursion cancelled?"

She shuffles her feet on the landing.

"No, that's the problem. Something has to be done for the few tourists who've made the effort to come here. There also has to be the right forecast," she adds.

"And is there tonight?"

"Yes, they were just phoning me from Northern Lights Ltd, and the forecast is good for the first time in many weeks."

She briefly shuts her eyes again. She looks wiped out after her night of work. Then she straightens up and says:

"All one needs is darkness and a clear sky."

I wait for her to come out with the favour.

"The question is whether you could take my place tonight."

She hesitates. "I heard you're on vacation until mid-January."

"Do you mean as a guide?"

"Yes, as a guide."

"In a coach?"

"Yes, you go in a coach. Otherwise it's not a northern lights excursion. You don't have to go far. Just far enough to escape the glow of the city lights."

I give it some thought.

"You sit in the front and speak into a microphone."

"What do I say?"

She takes a deep breath.

"You explain that the sun emits charged particles that escape into the Earth's magnetic field near the poles, where they move at great speed along spiral-shaped paths, stimulating molecules in the atmosphere, which emit energy that appears as the northern lights."

She shuts her eyes again.

"Yeah, or southern lights at the South Pole."

She pauses briefly.

"You then have to explain that the green and violet colours stem from excited oxygen and excited nitrogen. On the way home you don't have to say anything," she ends up saying.

When my midwife colleague has gone home to lie down, I knock on the loft door. I cut straight to the point and ask my neighbour if I can invite him on a northern lights excursion.

"We leave tonight at eight. That's if you're free," I add.

He looks at me.

"Yes, thanks, I'd love to."

The road ahead is bathed in light

There is a breeze in the air and a pale blue ring around the moon, but apart from the starlit sky, the world is black. The driver gives me a nod and introduces himself. He's in a fleece jumper marked with the company's name.

"Bragi Raymond."

I ask him about his name and he says it's run in the family for a long time; he has an uncle called Raymond Bragi and there are also several Gísli Raymonds. After giving it some thought, he rattles off the names of Styrmir Raymond, Búi Raymond and Samúel Raymond.

He then turns to the excursion plan and says that, even though the weather forecast is good, one can never be sure with the northern lights and we might need to go hunting for them. I tell him where I was intending to go and he says that's further than usual. I haven't travelled around the country much in the winter when it looks like a dis-coloured Polaroid snapshot, but as we're driving through the outskirts, the driver tells me I'm not the first midwife to accompany him on a trip and that he has also worked with several nurses. First aid knowledge is a requirement so it's therefore good to have a healthcare professional on board, he adds. He also tells me he has four daughters and that the first birth was the most difficult, but the others went smoothly. He himself had been delivered with a Caesarean section.

"Before I started driving tourists around, I worked in the fire brigade and drove an ambulance," the driver continues.

He says that on three occasions he assisted in the delivery of babies who were in a hurry to be born into the world in the ambulance: once at a bus shelter by Miklubraut, another at IKEA in Garðabær and a third time by a bakery not far from the National Library. But now he gets to see some landscape instead of handling accidents and fires.

There are patches of ice on the road and holes in the asphalt in many places and the driver often has to slow down.

He is silent for a while and then picks up the conversation again.

"I think to myself, could I be a farmer? It would be good to be able to produce one's own food when the next world plague strikes, but the answer is I don't know. There are so many things one doesn't know. In this job you meet people who've travelled all over the world and you ask yourself, what have they gained from it? I try to see what people are made of."

As he talks, his gaze is fixed ahead and he doesn't look at me. Finally, I tell him to pull over to the side of the road and I bend over to pick up the microphone. One can just about make out the mottled earth and snowdrifts in the lava field against the glare of headlights. He stops the coach and reminds me to tell people to be careful when they step off the bus. The passengers slowly vacate the semi-empty coach and cautiously step outside. They pause hesitantly on the penultimate step a moment, and breathe in the cold air. It's pitch dark and fiercely cold.

"Tell them not to stray too far from the coach," the driver says to me. "And that they should stick together in a group."

There is a sudden hail shower as I walk ahead with the group behind me in a single file, their hot breath painting the darkness grey. The driver is the last one to step out, bare-headed and bare-handed, in his fleece sweater. A short distance away, three horses press together with frost on their manes. The edge of the ravine is lined with frozen birch groves, deep below there is glowing magma. The tourists stand in a huddle in the middle of black rocks, a stone's throw from the coach and gaze up at the sky, waiting for the hail to stop, the heavens to open up and the flickering colour spectacle to appear in the upper atmosphere. They're ready with their cameras.

My neighbour from the loft hands me his gloves.

I smile at him.

Mother of the northern lights

The tourists climb back onto the coach and sink into their seats. They sit silently in their down parkas and hats and scarves wrapped around their necks.

"Was this your first trip?" the driver later asks.

I tell him it was.

"You took an unusual approach," he said. "I hadn't realized there were that many stars, how many did you say?"

"Five hundred and sixty thousand."

"And how many galaxies do we know of, you say?"

"Two hundred billion."

He is pensive for a moment.

"I've never heard a guide talk about electricity the way you did."

He turns up the heating.

"I thought it was quite striking when you spoke about your foremothers, the midwives, who travelled alone in the heart of winter in all weather, and how some of them lost their bearings and disappeared into the zone between heaven and earth and sometimes found their way and sometimes not. And it touched me when you said that the best time of the year to understand light was when there was the least of it. But I'm not sure that everyone got the analogy when you said that man grows in the dark like a potato. I noticed that many people nodded off on the way home, but I was awake because I'm the driver and listened to you. I have to admit, though, that I'd never heard a guide say that a person never recovers from being born. How was it you put it again? That the most difficult thing was getting used to the light? I don't think they all got that."

He sinks into a silence as we drive across Ártúnsbrekka back into town.

"One doesn't always see the northern lights on northern lights excursions," he finally says: "As a husband and father of four daughters, I'll always stand up for the midwife of the northern lights when tourists complain about not seeing the aurora borealis. And also because I'm a man. As true as my name is Bragi Raymond."

Behold, dawn breaks

Dawn is slow to break. Finally, a blue strip of daylight appears in the sky over the cemetery, and gradually widens and frosted leaves glitter on the graves. I get up and plug in the fast-boil kettle. The plug is working now. A text message from the electrician awaits me.

Sædís is feeling better
she is out in the garden
making a beautifully formed
white angel in the snow shaped like an hourglass

I open the window, take a deep breath, and fill my lungs with cold air.

The sun is enveloped in a veil of thin mist. I close my eyes and feel a faint glow, a slight warmth, almost imperceptible, from the golden globe on my eyelids.

You can come now,   day,

I am waiting   for you

to   rise

everything   is   white
everything   is   blank   and   empty

the   light   on   the   computer   screen   fuses
with   the   snowlight   outside

I   am   waiting

under   a   new   sky

f o r   a   n e w   e a r t h
to be born

a   b i r d
i s
h   e   a   r   d